Billy Above the Roofs

a novel in stories

by

Bob Ross

STEPHEN F. AUSTIN STATE UNIVERSITY PRESS

Printed in the United States of America
For information about permission to reproduce selections from this book,
contact permissions:

Stephen F. Austin State University Press
P.O. Box 13007, SFA Station
Nacogdoches, TX 75962
sfapress@sfasu.edu
936-468-1078

Project Manager: Kimberly Verhines
Cover Art: "Burwell Nebraska" by Joel Sartore
ISBN: 978-1-62288-914-3

1st Printing

This book of fiction is dedicated to:

Bud Alberts
Don Davis
Neil Fernau
Floyd Gould
Bee Graff
Howard Hitchcock
Glenn Masters
Sid Salzman
Gerald Skinner
Shep Strand
Reub Walton
Gene Welke
Glenn Weyer
Bob Zwiebel

—Friends of Edwin F. Ross
—Jokers, Historians, Troubadours

CONTENTS

Saint Billy

AFTER BILLY DIXON'S hilltop suicide, Ellen McDonough revised her recollections. Rather than a sly and secretive boy whom maturity had not improved, she remembered Billy as promising but flawed, a tragic victim of the Korean conflict. In death he became a pet of hers, a topic that came up from time to time. She even set up a scholarship in his name, to give high-school kids whom she felt to be deserving some money for college.

Her husband Rudy kept his mouth shut and reserved judgment.

The population of Turtle Lodge continued to decline. A new constable was found. Gerard Horse Looking stayed sober and took a job cleaning floors at the bank. He also polished the boards at the Pleasant Hour Lanes and Tables. He continued to be a nighttime presence in the town.

The people who lived south of the railroad tracks commemorated Billy in their own way by unofficially renaming Turtle Lodge Butte. They began calling it Mount Billy.

Very early one midsummer's day, a boy who was not afraid of snakes climbed Mount Billy to look out over the plains. It was the coolest hour of the morning—reptiles are less active then—and the sun's flat chin rested on the horizon. A flock of buzzards shook out their wings at one another in the thicket of Eastern redcedar that grew in despite of the lightning that probed the butte.

The sun gleamed red on the rails of the Cowboy Line. The baritone throb of a cattle truck weighted the air, accompanied by the bawling of steers. The boy's father knew the owner of the trucking company and could have gotten his son a job hauling cattle to the Iowa feedlots. The boy had a sweetheart, too, a tall ranch girl with man-sized hands and a generous heart. She would marry him if he asked her. He could stay and make a life in Turtle Lodge.

The sun was higher now, a ball of yellow fire that swirled if a person stared at it. He knew not to do this, although something east pulled at his mind. There was a university he could attend—he had gotten one of those Billy Dixon scholarships—and there were things to be known. His girl would find somebody else. She would waste no time about it.

Other boys read *Car and Driver.* He read Chaucer. It hadn't been easy getting the meter into his head, but his English teacher showed him the pronunciation, and he figured out the lines as best he could. He couldn't quite tell what he liked about it. Something about life, how it hadn't changed. *Gladly wolde he lerne and gladly teche.* His English teacher was like that. The miller who batted down doors with his head was a Hudspeth. The Wife of Bath lived in Turtle Lodge, too, wearing out her fourth husband.

More. There was more out there. Not only in books.

He had worked on a ranch the previous summer, driving a tractor around and around while the mower clacked and the grouse, if they were lucky, flew up ahead of the cutter bar. The man mowing on the opposite side of the field was fifty years old and a divorced grandfather. He knew everything there was to know about putting up hay.

The day warmed. One by one, the squabbling buzzards lumbered into the air. It was time to go back down the rugged trail. He would have to watch where he placed his feet, not only for the snakes. If a person once started to slide, he could end up at the bottom quicker than he expected. More people had been hurt going down than had been hurt climbing. Halfway down the path a rattler buzzed at him. He saw it coiled a little way off the trail. Its noise made his hair prickle, but he was in no danger from it. It was the one he didn't hear or see that bit him on the hand.

The pain was astonishing. He made it on down to his car and drove straight to the hospital. Luckily it was on the near side of town. The nurses didn't act surprised as he stumbled in the door, holding his hand out as if it were an offering. He would have let them cut it off, the pain was that intense, but they lanced the bite and gave him antivenin and a little morphine. The pain kept on as fiercely as before, but he felt more relaxed about it. They sat him in a vacant exam room and took turns looking in on him.

Pain traveled up his arm until he ached from wrist to shoulder and down into his chest. He felt alternately cold and hot, and his heart slammed. Now his neck hurt; now his head began to throb. He felt dizzy. He breathed deeply to calm himself and wondered if he would die. Maybe he should marry his ranch girl after all. If he lived. If his arm wasn't paralyzed. He guessed he could operate a tractor with one arm.

He could turn the pages of a book with one arm, too.

The nurse came in, a chestnut-haired, curly-haired woman who drove in every day from twenty miles south of Turtle Lodge. Her husband was the same deaf rancher the boy had worked for. He was six and a half feet tall and a steady drinker. One of the tightwad millionaires from down in the ranch country.

"How are you feeling? Does your arm hurt? Do you need more morphine?" She bent to poke at his hand; the rich brown of her hair concealed a gray layer near her scalp.

The boy grimaced. "It hurts like hell," he said. "No more morphine. I'm woozy enough, as is."

"We see a fair amount of snake bites," she said. "Haven't lost anybody yet."

"This must have been a big one. I never saw it."

"The half-grown ones are the worst," she said. "I suppose they put more poison in you because they're scared."

"Is Judy getting ready for college?" Judy was the couple's only daughter. A nice-enough girl to talk to, she carried a reputation as the town pump.

"Judy's waitressing," the nurse said. "I don't know what else she's doing. I never see her." A sadness crossed her face. "You young people," she said with a smile. "You need to get out of here. How is it now?"

The pain in his arm was less, and his heart had calmed. "I think I'm

3

going to make it," he said. "That bite was something else, though."

"What were you doing up on Mount Billy at seven o'clock in the morning? Were you on a vision quest?"

"Just trying to get a little perspective. I got more than I wanted."

"They say you can see five towns on a clear night. I've not been up there."

"I want to see more than five towns. I want to go to Europe."

"Good for you," the woman said. "Make sure they're not having a war when you get there. I think I hear Doc Cameron calling me."

"Is he going to look at me this morning?"

"He'll see you, but it might not be before eleven. I'll sneak you in something to read."

That was it, the big snakebite drama. It consisted mostly of sitting in a cold room. There wasn't enough to make a good short story. Of course his folks weren't happy when they got the bill.

The boy went on to become a college professor. He never forgot the kindness of Ellen McDonough and the little money she gave him from the Billy Dixon Fund. But the truth of the matter was, he scarcely saw any of them again.

He saw quite a lot of Europe; he saw St. Petersburg and the Louvre. But he never saw creaking buzzards take off from a twisted cedar tree, while the cold steel rails shone like copper and he could hear every sweet-voiced meadowlark within a mile.

His hand never fully recovered. It was difficult for him to turn a screwdriver or direct a pen. He came to be an excellent typist, a skill that served him well once personal computers had taken over the academic world.

He continued to love his Chaucer. His favorite lines were the innkeeper's, which he spoke (to himself) quite regularly at English department meetings: "'By God,' quod he, 'for pleynly, at a word/Thy drasty rymyng is nat worth a toord!'" He had few close friends in the department, none of whom were poets.

Yellowstone

I.

THE SECOND TIME Billy Dixon fell in love, it was with an automobile. *Zephyr* brought to mind lilacs and the smell of rain, and *Lincoln* was the Nebraska town he'd grown up in. *Lincoln Zephyr.* The paint color matched his pretty cousin's jade-green eyes.

The salesman bustled out to run him off. "Them hubcaps don't fit your car, kid," he said. "Beat it. I want you out of here." March mud was on his shoes.

"Don't own a car."

"How old did you say you was?"

"Seventeen." Billy, just turned sixteen, was a sophomore in high school, but the car salesman had to tilt his head back to look up at him.

"You got to be eighteen to buy a car," the man said. "Bring your mother with you next time, if you got one."

"She doesn't drive," Billy said. "I'm the one who needs a car."

"You got you a job?"

"I might get a better one," Billy said. "If I can get transportation."

"What did you say your name was?"

"William Franklin," Billy Dixon said. Too many residents of Lincoln knew his father. Walt Dixon stood out above a crowd like an upright bear.

"She's a beauty," the salesman said with a knowing wink. "Not every young fellow drives a car with these type of lines. Lemme show you what that V-12 engine looks like." He lifted the hood with a pair of red and stubby hands to reveal two long, bolt-studded cylinder banks with six exposed spark plugs standing upright on each. A big two-barrel carb sat far back; steel tubes curved up from the distributor to hold the wiring off the block. The engine looked clean except for a seep of oil under one of the cylinder heads.

Cold wind cut through Billy's jacket. "How many miles?"

"A little over thirty thousand. She sat up on blocks with the wheels off from nineteen forty-one to forty-six."

"Amazing," Billy said. *So why*, he continued to himself, *is it sitting on dirt at the back of the lot?*

THAT NIGHT AT the supper table, he put the question to his brother Frank.

"Them Lincoln vee-thwelf enginve iv a pfeefe of crapf," his brother said. Frank sat next to the empty space at the head of the table. Their father was away for the night, sorting mail on the Denver train.

"Why's that? Ford V-8s are pretty good."

"No they ain't. Them vee-thwelf iv worfe. Fumfin' wrong wif 'em from the facthry. Onfe they heatf up an' ftartf burnin' oil, they go to hell faft."

"How do you come to know this?" Billy asked, carefully eyeing his brother's gritty fists, clenched around the silverware.

"I juft do. At the fop, we're a bunf of expertf on ritf people've fit."

"I wish you boys would not talk dirty at the supper table," their mother said.

"Ma, I wav juft fayin'," Frank replied.

"I don't care. It's terrible," their mother said. "You're all half-civilized."

Billy went out into the front yard after supper. The house sat facing south, more than halfway up Belmont Hill, and below him Lincoln sparkled in its streetlight jewelry. The sea of lights broke where Salt Creek divided lower Belmont from the Russian Bottoms. The dark swath ran northeast to where his brother labored, over in Havelock where smokestacks above the Burlington shops trailed wisps of vapor. To the west, a "flying boxcar" droned on final approach to the air base. Ruth was out there, west of where the sun had just gone down, two hundred miles deep in nowhere country, stuck in a shit town and married to her truck-driver war hero. Billy prayed every night that his truck would slam into a bridge.

They were half-first cousins. Ruth was older by five years. They'd been lovers during the summer of his thirteenth birthday.

Billy turned back east toward the Burlington stacks. All Dixons felt the pull of the CB&Q. McFerrins and Cates did other kinds of jobs, but the Dixon men either hoboed or railroaded. His brother Frank hammered steel in the shops; his oldest sister had married a brakeman. His father wore a postman's uniform and got paid by the U. S. Government, but he rode the Burlington five nights a week, sorting westbound mail to Denver one night and eastbound mail to Lincoln the next. He spent half his weekends in Lincoln and half in Denver.

The only time Billy's father spoke to them was to tell them to turn off the radio. When he wanted to hear some music, he played the piano.

BILLY STOOD BACK to study the Zephyr's lines: sharp prow with a boatlike upsweep, rounded fenders shaped to breast-curves with chrome-and-glass nipples. It was a two-door, three-window coupe with no room for back-seat riders. An oil spot darkened the concrete under the engine.

"I thought you was going to bring your mother."

"Mom doesn't drive. I told you." The tailpipe was black, but the tires were new Fisk whitewalls. "How much?" Billy asked. "If I'm going to rob a bank, I need to know how much to get."

"Eight hundred," the salesman said. "Last year I could've got twice that for it. What'd you say your name was?"

"Wilson," Billy said. "Edward Wilson." The salesman didn't bat an eye. Evidently he was not exceptional when it came to memory.

Two long bus rides and a walk took Billy back west through downtown Lincoln, then north along 14th Street. He hurried to reach his school just as it let out. Bare-legged girls in heavy coats walked up the hill from Belmont High, and two of them made a point of looking back at him. Billy ignored them. Narrow in the hips and broad in the shoulders, clean-featured except for his suture, he knew himself to be handsome because Ruth had told him so. It was the Belmont girls who didn't measure up.

His sister Irma walked among them. Pert and not marked with the harelip, she'd been sneaking out to date a man in his twenties, an ex-soldier going to the University on the G.I. Bill. "You cut school again," she said. "I'm going to tell Ma."

"You know you won't," Billy said. "What did you learn in World History? In case I have to come up with something."

"Attila the Hun got thrown off his horse. Sally Nixon broke up with her boyfriend. Mr. Boesen's zipper was halfway down and nobody told him."

"I've been looking at a car," Billy said. "I'm going to take it for a test drive. Want to go for a ride?"

"You don't even have your license," she said. "You're lying as usual."

"Don't judge others by yourself," Billy said. "It's a big old Lincoln Zephyr."

"That's another fib," she said. "The only car you can afford is a broken-down Model T."

Billy earned pocket money getting up at four to stoke the coal-fired boiler at the high school. Every weekday morning, he walked a mile down to the school and a mile back up the hill once he got the fire refreshed. Most times he fell asleep at the kitchen table while he waited for his hot cereal. He didn't mind those first two miles, but the third mile—back down to attend class—felt like the Bataan Death March. Algebra meant nothing to him. You shoved letters around on the page, and if you got them in the right position, happy day! The answer popped out. Social Studies was worse. English was the worst because it came before lunch. He always slept through English, no matter what.

Billy never went to bed early because his mind tormented him. Ruth had shown him how to masturbate—that was how they'd started—and he couldn't close his eyes without remembering her cigarette-flavored kisses and her cool fingers on his shaft. That would have been all right, except that he shared an upstairs room with Frank. Frank would have noticed anything that might be used against his brother.

A LETTER HAD come addressed to Alice Mortensen Dixon. The Denver address had been heavily penciled through, and the letter had been redirected to Lincoln by someone other than his father. Billy found it in the mailbox and hid it to read later. It turned out to be a note from Sears & Roebuck, saying that a pair of size sixteen shoes had been back-ordered. Billy had never heard of any Dixons living in Denver. His father's aunt Clothilde lived in a creaking old house that faced 14th Street halfway down the hill. Aunt Clothilde was a Franklin. Ruth and her sister Ellen up in Turtle Lodge were Cates, but their older half-siblings were McFerrins. Billy's mother was a McFerrin, and the Franklins and the McFerrins were as close as two halves of a peach pit. Of these interrelated clans, the Dixons were most afflicted with the harelip. There was currently a Dixon in the state pen for burglary. If the crime had been auto theft, it would've been a Cate or one of the McFerrins. There had been no homicides in Billy's lifetime, though the clans' members had murdered one another pretty freely back in Ohio before the Civil War.

Billy lived through another night without seeing or tasting Ruth, while his father's snores rattled the windowpanes. He dragged himself out of bed before dawn to re-fire the boiler. At the school, the janitor-and-maintenance-man had left a pair of needle-nosed pliers on the basement floor, and Billy scooped them up. He already owned a screwdriver, courtesy of his brother's toolbox. Back at the Dixon farmhouse, he hid the pliers in his secret niche beneath the porch and went in to take his breakfast of lukewarm Cream of Wheat.

His father sat like a storm cloud at the head of the table. "What's the matter with *you?*" the huge man rumbled. "You look like you've been up to something."

"Good morning, Pa," Billy responded. "The janitor dropped some pliers. I put them on his bench."

"You better." The old man scowled. "If I hear of you getting in trouble, I'll whale the tar out of you."

Billy glanced at his sister Irma, whom he judged had slipped out again. The windows of the house on Belmont Hill leaked teenagers the way a broken engine block leaks anti-freeze.

This time he waited until school was out to visit the Zephyr. "Show me how you lift up the hood," he said to the salesman. "I want to see it run."

"You ain't showed me any money," the man complained. His words carried the scent of peppermints and whiskey. The latch held no secrets—the chrome ornament doubled as a handle—and the hood lifted smoothly and cheerfully, like the jaw of a hippo. Billy noted the wires, solid black to the ignition coil and yellow-with-a-black-stripe to the horn. The horn wire was big, meaning it carried a good amount of current, enough to spark the engine.

The salesman shoved the key into the switch and punched a chrome button on the dash. The starter turned the engine over, but it failed to fire. He pulled out the choke and pumped the footfeed. "She starts with a solenoid," he said. "You don't have to stomp a contact on the floor."

"You'll have to explain how that works," Billy said. "I've never seen one of those."

The engine caught and ran as smooth as cream. The salesman raised his voice. "You ain't seen a modern car, then. This one even has turn signals."

Billy drifted down the line of cars, pretending to look at two prewar Chevys, but nothing made his heart skip like the Zephyr. The salesman locked the office shack at five past six. "What time do you open in the morning?" Billy asked.

"Nine a.m.," the salesman said. "If it was up to me, it'd be two in the afternoon. I need you to clear out, sonny. It's quitting time."

The corn stubble on the other side of 48th Street showed a few green weeds. It was a chilly walk south to the bus stop on O Street. The bus lurched and stalled in traffic; Billy watched out the window as a young man in a suit jacket drove a maroon-colored Mercury whose flowing lines mimicked the Zephyr. On the curb side, the bus passed a black Ford car with white doors, parked behind a Model A pickup truck. The farmer beside the Model A had the hood cocked to one side. He and the cop were arguing.

Billy's father was on schedule to spend the forthcoming weekend in Denver. Billy calculated that if he left Lincoln before daylight, he could make it to Denver by nightfall and locate the address on the envelope. Whoever Alice Mortensen Dixon was, she would know where his father boarded and what he did, if she had ordered him a pair of shoes. On Sunday, once he'd satisfied his curiosity in Denver, Billy planned to drive back north to Turtle Lodge, Nebraska, and kidnap his cousin Ruth. (She would guess that he'd stolen the Zephyr, but she might still get in with him.) True, she had that damned kid now, but he intended to abduct her anyway. They would head out west to Oregon or California and start a life apart from all that family history. On the way west, they would drive through Yellowstone Park. He took the notion for a park visit from a calendar. His father got the family a brand-new railroad calendar every year at Christmas.

To be safe on his drive to Denver, Billy needed a valid set of license plates. His ancient great-aunt Clothilde lived on 14th, just up the hill from the school; she kept her Chevrolet locked in her garage, but she always paid for a set of current plates, so Billy stopped by to see her on Thursday after his classes, on the pretext that he wanted to borrow a shovel. If she'd left him alone in the garage, he could've taken her plates in an eyeblink, but she refused him the shovel and watched him from her front window until he left the premises. Farther down 14th Street, a few blocks past the school, there was a mechanic's shop protected by a German shepherd. Cars left outdoors there had plates, but Billy had no gift for taming junkyard dogs. He let the license-plate issue go unresolved for the time being. The best time to steal plates off a stranger's car would be early Saturday, just before he needed them.

On his way up the hill from Clothilde's he passed the Jewish cemetery, with their six-pointed star on the arch above the gates and two more on the gates themselves. His English teacher, Klein, was a Jew. Billy had read that in the new country of Israel, Jews didn't drive their cars on Saturday. If this Klein person didn't drive on Saturday, he wouldn't notice that his plates were missing. His address would surely be in the phone book.

Next place up from the cemetery was the Goat Lady's place. Across 14th Street to Billy's right was a cow pasture belonging to his father. The old man said land on the north side of Lincoln would be worth a lot of money some day. He kept the family poor buying vacant lots at tax sales, and spent his spare time fixing up old houses.

WHEN BILLY LEFT the house to stoke the boiler Friday morning, he had to step over his brother at the foot of the porch. Frank's face was bloody from one of his I. W. W. meetings, and a haze of alcohol and bitterness rose off him. Farther down, at the mouth of the driveway, his Crosley car sat in the ditch. Billy went back inside and got his brother a blanket before continuing down the hill, past the cow pasture, the Goat Lady's place, the cemetery, and Clothilde's.

The only thing different about Friday was that Billy stayed awake in English class, trying to guess if Klein was the type of Jew who wouldn't drive his car on Saturday. A fluffy-headed girl in glasses read a poem about the statue of some old giant: *Look on my works ye Mighty, and despair!* Among his father's mighty works was a half-mile ditch he'd dug to connect their farmhouse to the city's water main.

That evening Billy stood in the yard and watched the streetlights twinkle. Beginning in a couple of months, the fireflies would be flashing. The air would be swimming with the smell of clover, and frogs would be singing in the road ditches. Late wasps would be drunk on mulberry juice from the tree that shaded the gate. Billy had climbed the tree to eat mulberries, but he'd never tasted alcohol in his life.

BILLY PASSED THE school in darkness. No smoke drifted from the tall brick chimney. He flexed his shoulders inside the tight-fitting sport jacket, an old one of Frank's. His bare wrists stung with cold, but walking would warm him up. He had four miles to cover before sunup. He had fine long legs, his aunts all said, perfect for a mail carrier.

He did not think a U. S. Postal Service uniform would inspire his cousin Ruth to lift her skirt.

Billy wore his Sunday clothes to make himself look older. He had on one of Frank's fedora hats. The needle-nosed pliers and screwdriver weighted his pocket. He'd brought along a cardboard suitcase, but as he passed the fairgrounds on his way to Holdrege Street, the handle came off the suitcase. No matter; it was light and small, and he was able to tuck it under his arm. Carrying a broken suitcase made him feel like a displaced person, and he began to regret the sport coat, which was not keeping him warm.

The sky was still dark, though the morning newspapers were out. It was a frosty three-mile walk from Belmont Hill to the residential address south of Ag Campus. Billy's English teacher lived in a two-story brick house, with one mid-size maple and a tipped-over tricycle in the yard. His Plymouth was backed all the way up the driveway, bumper nearly against the garage. Billy removed the screws that held the license plates and pocketed them, and slipped the plates into a paper bag and put them in his suitcase. He didn't suppose it was a felony to take a pair of license plates.

From the English teacher's it was five short blocks to 48th Street, then half a mile south to the used-car lot. Billy flexed his aching arm after he set the suitcase down; then he got out the Plymouth's plates and lined them up in the Zephyr's holders. The needle-nosed pliers weren't much help, but his fingers were strong enough to hold the screws. The next thing was to start the car. Of course the doors were locked, but he'd brought clothes-hanger wire to lift the latch. He was more concerned about the state of the battery. If the Zephyr wouldn't start, he'd've had a long cold walk for nothing.

He opened the hood and rewired the horn wire to the ignition coil, then got inside with little trouble and twisted the cap off the steering column. He unscrewed the hot wire and shifted it to the opposite contact, then tightened the second screw and replaced the cap. Pull the choke out. Pump the gas. A person didn't want to pump too many times. He didn't know the Zephyr's magic formula. His heart in his throat, he pushed the starter button, and the engine turned, arr arr arr. On the second try it chugged and shook to life. The eastern sky was pink now, and there was enough light for him to see a faint blue cloud drift behind the car. Billy disapproved of stealing—he'd thought about going into police work as a career—and stealing the Zephyr would not be the end of it. The gas gauge showed barely a quarter-tank. Eighteen dollars wouldn't get him all the way to Denver and north from Denver up to Turtle Lodge, never mind to Yellowstone Park. He'd have to steal gasoline more than once along the way.

He was about to pull onto 48th Street when he spotted his broken suitcase in the rear-view mirror. He stopped and set the brake and ran and got it. He had to stow it behind the seat because the trunk was locked and he had no key to unlock it.

Gasoline was still on his mind as he approached the big new truck stop on West O Street. He hadn't thought that buying gas would be a problem, but now he realized that if the pump attendant saw him fiddling with the horn wire—the attendant would ask him to turn off the ignition, and he had no other way to do it—his road trip would end in the Lancaster County jail. Luck met him in the restaurant parking lot in the form of a five-gallon can of gas and a funnel in the open back of a farmer's pickup truck. Billy set the full can on the Zephyr's passenger's seat and cleared out for the next intersection, where he turned north onto a county road that passed the Air Force base. He drove west on Highway 34 to Seward and found a café, where he ordered coffee and pancakes and sausages. They weren't the cheapest items on the menu, but because he was driving a Lincoln Zephyr now, he ate like a prince.

FULL DAYLIGHT FOUND Billy heading west toward York, Nebraska, passing muddy-bellied cows in muddy cornfields. He grinned at the rear-view to check if his teeth were clean. Ruth said it was important to have good teeth if you wanted to get a screen test out in Hollywood. He returned his eyes to the road in time to correct a swerve. No highway patrolmen would be looking for him yet—he calculated that the salesman wouldn't miss the Zephyr for another fifty miles—but he reminded himself to pay attention to his driving.

He was nowhere near to running out of gas, but he wanted to get the tank filled just the same. He found a quiet street near the York Funeral Home, and parked and emptied the farmer's five-gallon can into the tank. Then he carried the gas can to a station down the block and filled it. The full can of gas was awkward to lug back, and he felt conspicuous lugging it. He decided that, once he got to Denver, he would rig a loop of wire to bypass the ignition. That way he could drive to the pump like a man who owned a Lincoln and order the attendant to fill 'er up.

Past York, he continued west on 34. His road turned south at Grand Island; then, at Hastings, it met with Highway 6 and began to angle southwest, running alongside the tracks of the CB&Q toward Holdrege and McCook. He thought of that other Zephyr, the crack passenger train that ran from Chicago to San Francisco. He planned to ride it one day, smoking a Havana cigar. One day when he could afford both train ticket and cigar.

He stopped in McCook and ordered a bowl of chili at a café near the railroad depot. The waitress, who looked to be about his age, wore a short cheerleader's skirt above fuzzy pants that hugged her legs. She re-lit a cigarette from an ash tray on the counter and studied him with mascara-crusted eyes. "You traveling, mister?"

"Denver," Billy mumbled with his mouth half full. The chili tasted wonderfully greasy.

"Get me out of this place," she whispered. "I'll pay half your gas."

"Can't," he said, telling half a truth. "It's not my car."

After he bought another five gallons, he found that his eighteen dollars had shrunk to twelve. He would have to eat bologna sandwiches the rest of the trip. The green car could not run on sandwiches, so he'd have to steal all his gas from then on or else spend more money. He could've taken the waitress's offer, but his nose wrinkled at the thought of her cigarettes—even though, now he came to think of it, Ruth smoked like a chimney and that was part of what he loved about her.

If he'd offered the waitress a ride, she'd have wanted him to sleep with her. A girl like that might give him a dose of clap.

LAIRD, COLORADO, WAS about the same as noplace, but it was the first town Billy had seen that was not in Nebraska. False-fronted businesses lined the highway like the set for a Western movie. The few people out on the town's main street turned their heads to stare after the Zephyr. Beyond lay naked wheatfields without trees.

The next town, Wray, looked more promising. Billy stopped at a grocery store to buy Wonder Bread and sandwich meat. He spent an extra dime and got a bottle of Dr. Pepper, then drank it on the curb and went back in to collect the deposit. "You rich boys got to watch your pennies," the male cashier said.

"Hunh?" Billy got caught off guard, until he remembered his Lincoln parked outside the store's plate glass. "That's right," he said, squaring his shoulders. "I have to save for college."

"College, hell," the cashier said. "You spend your allowance on pussy."

Once past the town, Billy turned in at a dusty airport and pulled up next to a new-looking Cadillac. He uncovered the horn wires to shut off the car and propped the door open to make his sandwiches. No planes were in the air, taking off or landing, but a man on the tarmac nearby was frowning at a low-wing Beechcraft. "Eighty-six octane!" he muttered, shaking his head. "What is the *matter* with these people?" Billy continued to munch his lunch meat and Wonder Bread. The man looked up. "You're Dr. Morrison's kid, am I right?" he said. "I thought I recognized that car. These morons here are trying to kill me. Again."

Billy swallowed thickly and took another bite, so the man would see that his mouth was too full to talk.

"You pay these pinheads God knows what," the angry man said, "and they just get stupider and stupider. Do you know what would happen if I tried to fly with 86-octane fuel?"

"That wouldn't be good, I guess," Billy offered.

"That wouldn't be good," the man agreed. "The heads would blow off the cylinders about the time I got off the ground. You got any room in your tank?"

"You mean my gas tank?" The man gave Billy a disgusted look. "Well, actually, I do."

"That's good," the man said. "I have to drain every drop of this crud out, and I hate to dump it on the asphalt."

If the man was surprised that Billy carried a gas can, he didn't say so. They used the can and a siphon hose to transfer gas from the airplane to the car. Once the Zephyr's tank was full, they filled the 5-gallon can a final time, and the man had Billy take a wing and help him roll the airplane into its hangar. "Can't make it to Estes before sundown," the man said. "I hate to fly over mountains when I can't see 'em."

"I don't blame you," Billy said, coiling the man's siphon hose, which he considered he now owned.

"Besides," the man said, "it's five o'clock and all these sons of bitches just went home, and I have to fill both wing tanks before I fly. Can I buy you dinner?"

"I already had a sandwich," Billy said. "I have to get going."

"Give my regards to the doctor," the man said. "Tell him it's time to trade in that old Lincoln. I can cut him a heck of a deal on a brand-new Oldsmobile."

The incident, besides being an unbelievable piece of luck, caused Billy to think about transportation. The silver Beechcraft could have gotten him to Denver from Lincoln in about four hours. If he'd stolen an airplane instead of a car, he'd be there now. But from Denver to Turtle Lodge? He didn't know if Ruth's town even had an airport. Probably all the planes they had up there were Piper Cubs that could land on a cow pasture.

At Culbertson, Nebraska, far behind him, Highways 6 and 34 had parted ways; now they rejoined at Brush, Colorado. Billy drove due west for an hour with his hand raised to block the sun. After another sixty miles, when the earliest stars were out, the road turned south-southwest. Long shadows streaked the cobalt sky; and low on the western horizon, blue-white peaks revealed the backbone of the continent. The snowy shadows brought to Billy's mind that up there it was winter. Midnight in the Mile-High City was going to be cold.

Soon the glow of far-off Denver rose ahead of him. The Zephyr hummed on airplane gas; he located the heater control and turned it up to High.

BILLY DID NOT own a watch, but when he saw the round clock in front of a suburban dentist's office, the time, 7:15, seemed early. He'd crossed over into Mountain Time. Where he'd come from it was 8:15, and he felt starved for anything that wasn't Wonder Bread and lunch meat. He passed a colorful restaurant that offered Mexican food, but he thought he'd best find out where his father boarded first, if for no better reason than to stay out of the old man's way. He had the envelope with the address belonging to Alice Mortensen Dixon. Since he did not know her at all, she surely wouldn't recognize him, and he could pretend to be a stranger returning the envelope. He hoped this aunt would be easier to get around than that suspicious old Clothilde.

Highway 6 turned into Larimer Street, and the stoplights began. As the lights changed to green and the Lincoln dragged up through the gears, Billy was passed at each stoplight by hot-rod cars driven by men his brother's age. Their exhaust pipes snarled and popped, and the drivers seemed to find the Zephyr comical. They swarmed around him, crowding his lane. He held the wheel steady to the next stoplight, where the driver of one of the hot-rods made a cranking motion for Billy to roll down his window. "Hey, Nebraska! Do you want to race, or fight?" The hot-rodder grinned above the stutter of his engine. His girl, a sulky blonde, nestled her face deep into the collar of his bomber jacket.

Billy held up the envelope. "Can you help me find Ogden Street? I'm looking for my dad's old aunt."

The hot-rodder's blue eyes went from Billy to the envelope. "Try down around the Capitol," he said. "Go to Colfax and turn left. Keep going and you'll come to it, baby face. After that, I think you better go home."

Colorado's state capitol building was hardly worth a glance. Billy supposed that, since they had mountains, they felt they didn't need an impressive capitol. He found Ogden Street and parallel-parked the Zephyr, and took a long minute to think about what he was going to do. He had stolen a car and driven it to Denver. Why? He intended to spy on his father. Why again? He mostly didn't give a damn what the old man did. By Belmont standards, Walt Dixon was an upright citizen. He fed the family and he didn't beat their mother, though none of his offspring was safe. There was never any money, but who in Belmont had money? Whatever the old tyrant did with his dough, he didn't drink it up. There was no valid reason to snoop, yet since Billy had found the letter, he'd felt pulled toward Denver the way a salmon is moved to swim upstream. He guessed it had something to do with Ruth. He hadn't missed the way the old man's eyes followed her. But Ruth's home was in Turtle Lodge, hundreds of miles from Denver.

Maybe when he saw this great-aunt of his, he would know why he had come.

Billy fumbled for the ignition key, then remembered he didn't have one. He twisted the cap off the column and disconnected the wires. Once he stepped out of the warm car, he immediately hunched his shoulders against the night air. He removed the envelope from his inner jacket pocket, studied it—though he'd memorized the address—and glanced up. The narrow little "shotgun" house was the lone wooden structure on a street of brick apartment buildings. Its front yard stood empty except for two small leafless trees, but though the porch was shabby and the narrow yard was bare, every calico-curtained window pulsed with light and warmth. A radio blasted polka music, and he could hear the happy play-shrieks of little kids being chased by a growling monster.

Whoever this person was, she was no Clothilde. Clothilde's house was always dark as the grave at night. This odd little shanty was lit up like a tavern.

Billy's step slowed as he drew closer. He checked the envelope again. The address was correct, but everything else was wrong. Bows of Easter ribbon fluttered on the door, and light poured extravagantly from every window. Along with the children's squeals came the yap of a claw-rattling terrier. If any Dixon from Lincoln or Havelock owned a dog, it would be a Doberman with torn ears and broken teeth.

Billy sidestepped the blocks of light that fell on the yard. Cautiously— so the yapper wouldn't hear him—he tiptoed to the edge of a window and peeked inside. There was a giant in the room who resembled his father, except that this giant was laughing. He carried a red-headed child on his shoulders and stomped his feet at the dog that barked and nipped his trousers. Two more children in pajamas, a boy and a girl, ducked in and out of the room; a woman came from the rear of the house, wearing a bright blue dress that had not been sewn from flour sacks, to scold them and order them to their beds (they did not comply). She came bustling back with a smile in her eyes, to pause and stand on tiptoe and give the giant a peck on his collar. She was pretty and plump and blonde and wore a wedding band.

Alice Mortensen Dixon.

Billy was so stunned that he stepped straight into the light. The giant glanced out the window; their eyes met, and before he had time to blink, the man became the father he had thought he knew.

"Billy! You little turd! Wait till I get hold of you!"

Billy bolted. His feet left the premises. He tripped on the edge of the sidewalk and heard a door slam behind him. He was up in an instant and off down the walk, past the Zephyr, past a white-haired man walking his poodle. "Billy!" a great voice roared behind him. "You get back here, God damn you! Billy!"

A woman's voice floated out of the darkness. "Walter! Walter, are you all right?" Billy paused in his flight to look back. His father stood still in the middle of the sidewalk, holding both hands to his chest.

"Billy?" He spoke the name wonderingly, as if he were waking from a dream. "Come back, boy." He tottered and collapsed. Billy imagined a mighty cloud of dust such as would rise from a fallen statue. Then he turned his back and ran for his life.

BILLY KNEW IT had to be Sunday morning. Something heavy and warm and scratchy was holding him down. A hard object kept punching his shoulder, jab jab jab. He twisted away to avoid it, but it wouldn't quit.

He opened his eyes a little. The hair in his mouth belonged to a black-haired girl in a man's Army-surplus overcoat. Silhouetted against a brilliant blue-white sky, a grinning cop was prodding him with a baton.

Billy's bare wrists smarted from the cold. He raised his head slowly off the bus bench. The girl jerked awake and looked up at the cop in fear. The mile-high world spun and rocked, and a headache fell on him like an avalanche. "It moo-ooves. It bree-eathes. It multipli-i-ies," the cop droned in a carnival barker's voice.

"Ouch," Billy said, struggling to sit up. "Don't poke me. I don't feel good."

"So, what brings a nice college boy to Five Points," the cop said, "besides cold beer and hot pussy?"

19

"I don't know this person," Billy said. "I never saw her before. Not until this minute."

"Sure you never," the grinning cop said. He had a sour-looking partner who stood aside. "Looks like the two of you was playing house on a bus bench. Did you give her money?" The girl sat up and looked around for her purse. She appeared to be thirteen or fourteen, all brown eyes and bones.

"I don't remember," Billy said. "I was trying to find my father."

"You must've been looking for him in a strip joint." The cop turned to the girl. "You," he said. "Vamoose. Scoot! Quick, before I run you in."

She reached for Billy's arm. "*Matrimonios*," she said.

"Nobody is *matrimonios*," the cop said. "Get your whorey little ass out of here before I kick it up between your tits."

The girl understood him well enough; anyway she left. Billy hung his pounding head. "I have to find Ogden Street," he said to the bench. "Do you think you could help me?"

"I might, but I ain't gonna carry you," the cop said. "Can you stand and walk?"

Billy stood and walked. He had never drunk liquor before; now he found out all at once what his brother Frank faced every Sunday. It was not so much that his head felt dynamited, or that his mouth stank like rotten grapefruit. More than those, it was a sense of death-like illness spreading outward from the marrow of his bones. To move his limbs in synchrony took an effort of concentration; he followed the cops by keeping his eyes fixed on their heels. When they stopped, he bumped into them. The talkative one placed his hand on a gray metal pole and looked up at the street sign. "Ogden Street."

"Thanks."

"Did she leave you your billfold? Better check."

"Who?" Billy's mind drew a blank. "Oh. The girl." He dragged out his wallet. The leather was empty except for his pictures and birth certificate.

"Thought so," the cop said. "Alan, you got any?"

"I'm not giving him nothing," the other one said. "He's probably some rich kid from up at Boulder."

"Come on," the first cop said. "He needs to get himself some breakfast. Otherwise he's gonna feel like crap all day." Between them, the cops gave Billy six dollars. "Don't ever let me catch you around Five Points," the first cop said. "You're lucky you didn't get your throat cut. If you'd been old enough to shave, I'd've took you to the lockup. Next time, I will."

Billy set off to follow Ogden Street, leaving the cops to enjoy their day. He had no recollection of where he'd parked the Zephyr, or of how far the little shotgun house was. He passed pawnshops, bookstores, brick apartment houses. The street did not look friendly or familiar. After he'd stumbled along for what seemed like half an hour, he glanced up and saw the green car facing him. He realized he'd already passed the narrow house, and he looked back over his shoulder, half expecting to see his father's corpse. The sidewalk was empty. In daylight, the house looked abandoned, the trees in front mere skeletons. The warmth that had shone from every window was gone.

Billy knelt beside the car to puke, but though he retched, nothing would come up. He hauled himself to his feet, opened the door, twisted the cap from the center of the steering wheel, and reconnected the wires. He pumped the gas, pulled out the choke, and pressed the chrome button. The V-12 engine thudded and clunked to life. It did not run as sweetly as the day before. He found Larimer Street and turned to put the morning sun on his right. The street was lined with used-car lots and gas stations. No hot-rodders cruised the stoplights. He passed a clapboard church, its parking lot still vacant. When he jammed on his brakes at the next stoplight, the lunch meat and Wonder Bread slid out from beneath the seat. He pulled over to the curb to retch again, and kicked the stale food out the door.

He'd been drunk already when he bought the girl a meal. He couldn't recall having sex with her, but maybe they had. On the bus bench? He squirmed at the thought. He and Ruth had had to do it in odd places, but they'd always managed to conceal themselves. He wondered if the black-haired girl was Mexican.

Ruth. Nebraska. Nebraska was where he was headed. He blinked and almost drove the car off the road.

BILLY STOLE FIVE gallons of gas from a church-going farmer. There were tire tracks in the yard, but only the dogs were at home. He stole five more gallons farther up the road. He understood that he was becoming careless. The Zephyr kept going, but a fool could tell it did not like the fuel. Evidently tractor gas took the hum out of airplane gas. In Brush, Colorado, where Highways 6 and 34 parted, he took a chance and bought clean gas from a station. He got himself a White Owl cigar and drank water, which made him wobble, though the cigar helped calm his stomach. He thought the car ran smoothly, more like itself.

He'd planned his trip by visualizing highway numbers, but his night in Denver had sandblasted them away. Billy knew he had to take the northern route out of Brush. He needed to cross Nebraska almost to the northern border, but the highways didn't go in that direction generally, so there had to be a lot of zigging and zagging; he got lost in a snarl of back-country roads. The sun crossed the meridian and his gas needle slid below a quarter tank. Finally he pulled to one side of the gravel road he was on and got out and sat on a fender, looking at nothing. A line out of English class came to him: *The lone and level sands stretch far away.* Except that the sands weren't level. The hills rolled away like the waves of a grass-covered sea.

When the light was almost gone, a man in a muddy pickup truck came along and asked Billy if he needed something. "Can you sell me five gallons of gas?" Billy said. "And show me how to get to the highway."

The rancher gave him gasoline for nothing. The nearest highway turned out to be Highway 2, running southeast and northwest. The rancher told him that if he followed it southeast, he would reach Grand Island in a couple of hours.

"Does it join up with Highway 34 at Grand Island?" Billy asked.

"Don't know," the rancher said. "Never been that far east. If there's something I can't find in Scottsbluff, I drive to Cheyenne."

Billy gave up going to Turtle Lodge to look for Ruth. It was a fool's errand anyway. His good shoes were destroyed, the car's tailpipe had begun to smoke, and his sport jacket was as rumpled as a hobo's handkerchief. His insides felt gritty and twisted, like a wool shirt that has had ditchwater wrung out of it. That was what his blood felt like: ditchwater.

He drove eastward past the glimmering streetlights of Broken Bow. Hours later, Highway 2 ended; he blundered south through Grand Island until he found the road that would take him east to Lincoln. Farther on, past the town of Aurora, the Zephyr rolled to a stop. He woke up in time to wrestle it to the shoulder. Steam boiled from underneath the hood.

Billy carried his broken suitcase back to the quiet town. He got a room at the first motel he came to, took a shower, and collapsed into bed. As near as he could tell, he felt exactly as ill and miserable as the hour he'd left Denver.

HE WAS AWAKENED by somebody pounding on the door. He opened it to find a Nebraska state highway patrolman blocking the light.

"Get your shit and come with me."

Billy put on his jacket and lifted his suitcase. He wished he'd been given ten seconds to wash his face.

The patrolman drove east a mile and pulled over behind the green car. "Know anything about this?"

"Nope," Billy said. "I was hitch-hiking."

"How come the dirt on your shoes matches the dirt on the floor mats?"

"Same roads, I guess."

"Don't dick with me, son," the patrolman said. "I'm not used to it." They sat in silence. "Well," the patrolman said at last. "What about it?"

"I was taking it back," Billy said. "The engine broke."

"Next time, steal a Buick." The patrolman started his black-and-white Ford car. "As it happens, I am driving back toward Lincoln," he said. "I know a man in Lincoln who wants to see you."

"I don't think anybody in Lincoln wants to see me."

"This man does. He's got a job offer for you. He's going to buy you a train ticket to San Diego. After you've been there a dozen weeks, you'll travel. You like to travel, don't you?"

Billy thought of the railroad calendar on his bedroom wall. Yellowstone. What difference did it make? "I don't care," he said at last. "Just don't take me home."

They drove on. "You know a fellow name of Frank Dixon?" the patrolman asked. He glanced at Billy and drew back his upper lip. "*Whorkerve of the whirl, unife and fife! You haf nuffing to loofe but your chainf, and a whirl to whin!*"

Billy rode in silence for another mile. "You'd better not make fun of my brother Frank," he said. "He will knock your head off."

II.

THAT, MORE OR less, was how Billy found himself on the slope of a mountain in Korea. The valley below him seethed with Chinese soldiers. Determined as ants, they attacked the hill in waves. He sat behind sandbags at the back of a .30-caliber machine gun, firing down on them as bullets whipped past his head.

The valley was deeply rounded like the bowl of a broken teapot, with a talus slope for the remnant of the spout. The Chinese had to climb the talus, and they weren't making it. The ones who followed took weapons from those who died and continued to scramble upward until they died, too. The machine gun was an efficient tool and kept hammering. He'd shot the rifling out of the barrel, but it didn't matter. If he failed to hit a man in front, he would hit the man behind him.

The Chinese quit coming after a while, and Billy used water from his canteen to cool the receiver. He wished he could afford to drink some. Dead Marines lay east and west of him above the talus. Some had carried full canteens, but he couldn't risk leaving his foxhole, even for a second.

Bugles blew downslope; he resumed firing. A corporal ran up to feed the belt, using his feet to shove a dead PFC out of the way. After the corporal was hit, Billy fed the gun himself. Another man brought up a box of ammo. At one point, the gun got hot and jammed. Billy poured water on the receiver, coaxed the bolt back, and extracted the shell. The clambering Chinese soldiers rattled the shale. He thrust a cleaning rod down the barrel and pulled it out, dribbled more water, repositioned the ammo belt. The bolt clicked into place and he triggered the Browning. The enemy fell like wheat.

The Chinese expended themselves in a kind of madness until none were left to fight. When the assault was finally over, their bodies lay in windrows. The few Marines who were able to stand stared at one another hollow-eyed. The only person of rank among them was a captain, nobody's favorite.

Rain began to fall. It mixed with blood and trickled down the slope. The living walked among the dead, firing occasionally. The captain used his big pistol to finish off survivors; other Chinese were rounded up in a circle, with a lone man guarding them. The Marines would be pulling out as soon as the trucks came. There was a useable one-lane road on the back side of the mountain.

Billy carried the hot machine gun by its handle, with the bolt pulled open to cool the steaming barrel. His feet seemed to glide a half-inch off the ground. The trail that led up to the talus slope flowed red. He avoided it. There was a feeling of time at a standstill, except when the captain's shots punctuated the silence. Even the blue-winged magpies that followed the troops were silent.

The captain stopped near Billy to reload. "Why are you not firing?" he asked. "Do you expect me to do this by myself?"

"With this?" Billy glanced down at his machine gun. "What happens to our guys who get taken prisoner? Won't the Chinks do the same to us?"

"You'd better hope that's all they do to you," the captain said. "You'd be better off dead than captured."

The captain continued to execute the wounded. Billy didn't see any point in machine-gunning them. He joined a group that was gathering Chinese weapons, mostly "burp" guns, to be piled and burned. There he found a light-skinned soldier with a type of weapon he hadn't seen, a new kind of submachine-gun carbine. The soldier wore foreign insignia, not Chinese. Billy would have liked to ask where he was from, but the man had gone cold and stiff. He removed the bayonet from the efficient-looking weapon and tucked it under his belt.

Dead Chinese soldiers lay scattered on the slope like logs. Children could have built a fort with their corpses. He remembered his beautiful cousin Ruth, and the thought of his great distance from her—her husky voice, her smooth, long, soft-skinned body—overwhelmed him. He pressed the muzzle of the weapon he was carrying to the tip of his right boot, over the third toe. He thumbed a single round into the chamber. He pulled the trigger.

The pain was stunning, but what was worse was the look of contempt in the captain's jade-green eyes.

In the Tunnel of Love

BILLY DIXON GRIPPED the window frame of Baldwin McDonough's pickup truck. Baldwin drove the truck in "regular low" gear as they bumped across the pasture and dropped down over a knoll. Five Hereford heifers, prized breeding stock that Baldwin had kept for replacements, lay stiff on their backs near a tie-down in the fence, their legs splayed straight out from their bodies. The morning sun shone brightly on their virgin udders, plumped with the bloat of death.

A thunderstorm had washed the sky to a clean ceramic blue, and a breeze from the north made green waves in the cheatgrass. Baldwin shut off his pickup and glared at the lightning-killed heifers. Clouds of flies worked their orifices; Billy held tight to the door handle and felt his stomach rise. He'd seen maggots at work in Korea, not on dead cattle.

"'Ey! You goi'nh help me, or you goi'nh listen to the God-da'n meadowlark?"

Baldwin spoke like a man lifting stones at the bottom of a well. Deciphering his speech wasn't easy, but Billy had grown up with a speech-impaired brother and understood Baldwin better than most could. He glanced at the older man's hearing aids and wondered what he knew about meadowlarks. According to Irene McDonough, Baldwin's wife, Baldwin

26

had been deafened at the age of ten, when he'd contracted scarlet fever. *Speak loudly and make sure that he's looking at you.* That was her rule. Billy had been advised not to play poker with him because, people said, he could read faces.

Baldwin's insurance-agent brother had already been out from town and given his OK to take the hides. Now the two men tugged the carcasses into a line, and Baldwin reached in through the pickup window and brought out two knives and a whetstone. One knife had a dark-brown blade whetted to a sliver. Copper harness rivets held the pitted steel to a fat, bleached cottonwood handle, hand-whittled and worn to a softness that was almost furry. The other was an ordinary kitchen knife with a bright stainless blade and a hard, slick ebony grip. Neither knife had a crossguard or a blood groove. Baldwin took longer to sharpen the first, but he grumbled more over the second.

He tucked the whetstone into his hip pocket and offered the newer knife to Billy. "I HAVE MY OWN," Billy said, and glanced toward his belt, where he carried a bayonet that he'd found on the battlefield, somewhere above Chosin Reservoir.

"Let' see it."

Billy slid his bayonet from the sheath he'd made for it and presented it grip-first toward Baldwin. "No good," the older man said. "Blade too straight for skinni'nh. Too heavy at the back. Your wrist ain't goi'nh last a half an hour."

"I PREFER THIS ONE." Billy felt his ears redden. Most men who saw his bayonet showed it more respect.

Baldwin shot him a gray-eyed look. "I guess you the knife expert. Done much skinni'nh?" Billy shrugged. "Watch me, now." Baldwin started the first carcass by cutting around a hock and slitting the inside skin of the hind leg. "Here." He slit the belly without puncturing the paunch, then cut around the twat and anus and down the underside of the tail. "An' like this aroun' here." He showed Billy how to do the neck. "Now you peel the hide. Feel OK?"

"I'LL BE FINE," Billy said.

"If you got to puke, don't forget which way the wind blowi'nh." Baldwin straightened, using the heifer's foreleg as a banister. He turned his long back on Billy and moved off to start the next heifer.

The bayonet's handle was broad and deeply grooved, with a tang forked to clip around a gunbarrel. It felt angular and awkward in the hand. Billy scrubbed the blade into the hide and made cuts inside the legs, along the underside of the tail, up the belly. When he began to peel the hide from the flesh, he released a fresh-meat smell that made the clean air thick to breathe. As he waited for the breeze to clear it away, a pair of Western kingbirds—"bee martins," according to Baldwin—chittered from the barbwire fence. Occasionally one would dart near Billy to snatch a fly.

Billy's progress was slow, but for once Baldwin didn't complain. In fact, the older man wasn't saying anything. Billy watched his employer from the corner of his eye. At first he would grip his rust-blackened sliver of a knife, working furiously as was his habit. Then he would slow to a standstill and pass his sleeve across his face. The rasp of his harsh breathing filled the swale.

Finally Baldwin stood to his full height and tested his knife edge with his thumb. He went to the truck and got the water jug and a shallow pan, and returned and made himself comfortable on an unskinned heifer. Billy stood up from his own work and crossed over to offer Baldwin the bayonet. "CAN YOU PLEASE TAKE A LOOK? THIS BLADE FEELS SHARP, BUT IT WON'T CUT."

Baldwin frowned at the bayonet and then tossed it back toward the truck, where it thunked against a fender and dropped down into the grass. "*I tol' you*," he gritted through plastic teeth. "*That blade no fuck'nh good.*" Billy's dismay must have registered, because the older man's eyes relented. "Maybe good for killi'nh Jap. No good for skinni'nh."

"IT'S FROM RUSSIA. MADE TO KILL AMERICANS." Billy turned to note where his bayonet had fallen, but instead of going to pick it up, he squatted to watch his boss whet the worn-down blade. The man's long hands made a careful ballet, *stroke stroke stroke stroke stroke* on one side, then a graceful dance that floated the blade above the stone and five equal strokes on the other. His motions seemed both in and out of character: efficient yet feminine.

Baldwin caught him looking. "I spose you think I sharpeni'nh like a sissy," he said. "I guess that' cause a woman show me how. Ol' Mary. She a mean one, too." He rinsed the knife in the water bucket and picked a fleck of tallow off the steel. Then he settled back and shook out a cigarette.

"I took me a job," Baldwin said after lighting up and exhaling. "January nineteen eighteen, winter after I lef' school. I skin sheep for ol' Howie Fredricksen." He pushed his hat back from his gleaming white forehead so it rested on the bulbs of his hearing aids.

"Fifteen a hell of an age," he said, and squinted down along the blade. "You ain't quite a man, but you ain't no child exactly, either. You ain't seen nothi'nh an' you can't do nothi'nh, but you know you 'bout as smart as the nex' fella.

"Howie los' hinself a bunch of sheep that winter. Had 'en pent up, too, but they bus' out an' pile up in a draw, ewe an' lamb together. Doesn' take no bad storm to kill sheep; they got a talen' for commiti'nh suicide." He paused in his sharpening to rinse the stone.

"Nineteen-seventeen an' eighteen, single men gone off to France. Grain price good, cattle price good, plenty of cash in the country.

"Ol' Howie talk money an' buy whiskey all up and down Main Street, but nobody got any sense want to skin then frozen sheep. Howie got to keep tryi'nh, though. One sheep die, you leave her for the coyote; couple hunnert die, hide four buck apiece, you take the skin.

"Here's me, finish corn picki'nh in December. Christmas an' New Year come an' gone, no work, no money, livi'nh on cracker and bean; sleepi'nh with the rat in the hay barn out back of the feed store, but I be damn if I'n goi'nh go back an' live off my folks. Here's Howie, scouri'nh street an' bar for skinner. All he can get is a couple of drifter an' Mary Lang." Baldwin tested the thin old knife with his thumb and put it aside. He picked up the newer one. "An' me. Speaki'nh of whiskey, you had a drink this morni'nh?"

"I DON'T DRINK WHISKEY."

"Me too neither." Baldwin carried the water jug to the pickup and dug a pint of Old Yellowstone from under the seat. He placed the bottle thoughtfully to his lips and tilted his head back. "Only once in a while." He offered the bottle to Billy, then capped it and sighed.

"Anyway," he said, "this here Mary an ol' gal come from down along the river. Wore bib overall, flannel shirt, always carry a can of snoose. Red hair, freckle face, kind of big woman. Don't act friendly, but people aroun' here kind of use to her. Might not even look so bad if she took a bath." Baldwin glanced at the heifers and at the sun and handed Billy the newer knife. "You can work while y' listeni'nh."

"Then two drifter, I didn' care for the way they look. Like a half-starve pair of houn' dog runni'nh the country. Ringo, they call thenselve; Larry an' Jerry Ringo. Black hair slick back, teeth rotten from bad whiskey. They think they plenty handsome, should've been movie star.

"Most rancher in then days still use a team an' wagon. Howie get his team hitch up aroun' four o'clock, load us all into his wagon under a robe. Then two Ringo about half looped, an' Mary Lang ain't no pinnacle of sobriety. We pack in alongside flour an' salt an' bacon an' bean, sugar an' coffee an' a crate of egg, an' away we go. Wind blowi'nh snow down our neck and coveri'nh our track." Baldwin helped himself to another swallow. He screwed the cap back on the bottle, stood and slid it under the pickup's seat, and moved to the carcass he'd been cutting on. "Cold an' snow suit Howie just fine, cause his skinni'nh crew won't leave.

"Already that first night, Howie had trouble with Mary Lang. She wouldn' sleep in the men bunkhouse, an' she refuse to sleep in the hay barn. Got to sleep in the house or else she goi'nh walk back to town. Miz Fredricksen wouldn' sleep in the house with Howie an' Mary both; says Howie tryi'nh to put one over, better take *her* to town. Howie says horses tired, he's tired, wagon ain't goi'nh nowhere. Ol' lady fire up an' chase Howie out of the kitchen. After supper—" Baldwin postponed work for a second, looking off down the breeze. "Me an' then two Ringo settle in to bunkhouse alongside Jake Mueller, ol' Howie herder. Door bust open an' here come Howie with a blanket, chewi'nh his mustache.

"'Come in, Owart,' Jake Mueller tells 'en. 'Ve put an extra chunk in der stove. Chust look, boys, der Pope come to bless his subchecks.'"

Billy had peeled one side of his animal down to the backbone. He'd smeared blood and tallow on his new Wrangler jeans. Baldwin, in spite of his cigarette and blah blah blah, had almost finished skinning his first carcass.

"Ol' Howie come in cussi'nh," Baldwin said. "He would of fire ol' Jake on the spot excep' he need every hand he got, and Jake the best.

"That night it blow an' drift right up to the windows. Next morni'nh too cold for skinner to work outdoor, so first thing we got to do is clear a space inside the sheep barn. Howie sheep barn nice an' big, got an alley down the middle for wagon; course the alley got pile full of junk over the year. We move most of it out so Mary Lang and then Ringo boy got room to work. Jake Mueller got all he can do to get hay out, try an' keep the rest of Howie sheep from starvi'nh, so that leave then Ringo boy an' Mary Lang to skin, twenny-five cent a hide. Me, I'n spose to get two dollar a day for helpi'nh Howie, worki'nh out in the wind, bringi'nh sheep carcass.

"Later on, I skin sheep instead of hauli'nh, but I still only got two dollar.

"Howie drove us all down to the gully an' we throw dead sheep on the wagon. Never did get a count, but there's a pile of 'en there, all frozen on top of one another.

"Kerosene stove no bigger'n a five-gallon bucket is the only heat in that barn, an' the stove only there to keep a pan of water hot so the skinner can sharpen they knive. Snow blowi'nh in between the board, pile up along the wall. No light but a couple of dirty window. Lantern hangi'nh on a nail, but ol' Howie just as tight as the wallpaper. Says they don't need to light no lantern in the daytine."

Baldwin had finished skinning his first heifer; Billy still labored over his. The older man eased his back, and chafed his arms and shivered in the sun. "Ride in with Howie an' a wagonload of frozen ewe," he said. "Jump off and run ahead, hurry up an' get the door shovel open. Then quick close the door behind 'en to keep the snow out.

"At first a man think he's in a railroad tunnel. After a while he'll see a gray pile, dead sheep that ain't been skin, an' a dark pile, bloody carcass. Maybe see a knife blade flashi'nh. Throw dead sheep on the first pile, drive wagon up, throw bloody carcass on. Chop snow an' push the secon' door open, drive back out into the light. Be cold an' dazzle an' blind all over again. You need help turni'nh that heifer?"

"I CAN GET IT."

"Don't know who said it first," Baldwin said, "but we start calli'nh that alley the Tunnel of Love."

BILLY DIXON STOOD six feet three inches tall, but he still had to tilt his head back when he spoke to Baldwin. He'd come into the country tough and lean from the Marines, but the older man outworked him every time. Billy had lived at the ranch three weeks, and he knew already he wouldn't last the summer. Besides, ranch work wasn't bringing him any closer to his cousin Ruth, who lived in Turtle Lodge, the principal town of the county.

His wrist turned and his blade cut a gash in the hide. "SHIT! THIS KNIFE IS DULL AGAIN."

"Eh?" Baldwin looked up from the third heifer, where he was making the initial cuts. Billy straightened and showed him the kitchen knife. Baldwin came and took it, examined the blade, and carried it over to the pickup. He sat on the tailgate and placed the pan of water beside him. He lit another cigarette and pushed back his hat.

"I CAN SHARPEN IT," Billy said.

"Use that good knife while I fix this one," Baldwin said. "Some people can sharpen knive. Other people, all they do is wear out whetstone.

"Then Ringo boy," he said, "they look like twin, excep' one of 'en a shrimp an' the other one tall. We call 'en Little Ringo an' Big Ringo. Both of 'en got bad teeth, small like baby teeth, black an' rotten in between. They couldn' eat no sugar.

"Big Ringo think he quite the man. His main subject of conversation is the women he screw an' how long his dick is."

"THAT'S TWO SUBJECTS."

Baldwin gave Billy a contemplative look. "First night they already complaini'nh. Too cold, skinni'nh sheep too hard. They need whiskey to warm 'en up. Howie ought to give 'en whiskey. Whiskey, whiskey, whiskey. Howie not too happy sleepi'nh out in the bunkhouse, Mary Lang nice an' toasty up at the house. He tell 'en they can shut up or go to hell, walk to town in the snow.

"Next day, then Ringo boy start a slowdown. Mary Lang skin more ewe than both of 'en put together. After supper ol' Howie let 'en know what he think about it—course, he want to get then sheep skin before the weather warm up— Well, he no more'n mention warm weather, an' Big Ringo go to braggi'nh 'bout his dick.

"Jake Mueller say, 'Ringvorm, effry chackass iss got a dick.' Big Ringo pull out his skinni'nh knife an' go to feeli'nh along the blade, an' it occur to us about that tine that we don't know then drifter. That bunkhouse getti'nh to feel a little bit crowded."

While Baldwin talked, the flies gathered. Billy had resumed skinning, although, like the Ringos, he was staging a slowdown. "SO THEN WHAT HAPPENED?"

"Nothi'nh." Baldwin came to hand over the gleaming kitchen knife and take back his precious relic. "Howie send ol' Jake out to check on ewe, an' while Jake gone Howie promise Big Ringo that if he work hard an' shut up about his dick, Howie throw in a jug of liquor with his paycheck."

Billy went back to skinning, half listening to Baldwin's yarn. When he'd first arrived from Korea, he'd gone straight to work for his cousin Ruth's husband, trucking cattle from the sandhills ranches. Every trip involved a morning stop for coffee, and the coffee drinkers each had a story about Mary Lang. There couldn't be much crime in Dunlap County, Billy reasoned, if they still talked about Mary Lang after forty years.

When he made the final cut along the backbone, the denuded carcass slid off its hide and onto the grass like a 600-pound bar of soap. Billy jumped out of the way. Baldwin laughed. The two men gripped the flayed beef by the tail and dragged the slick body to one side. Baldwin turned to the half-peeled heifer he'd begun and slapped her upturned hock. "You finish this'n," he said. "I'll start the next."

Billy straddled the half-skinned heifer's neck and began pulling the hide away from the meat. Baldwin's Herefords each carried the breed's distinctive "shawl:" red-yellow along the sides of the neck, white at the throat and along the spine. Pretty, if a person liked cattle. Billy had not liked trucking them. They shit tons, literally, and he hated the thought of working for his cousin's husband. After he'd met Baldwin through Ruth, actually through Ruth's sister, he'd thought he might learn the cattle business and grow rich. It didn't appear Baldwin was going to teach him how to get rich, and besides, being a rancher was unattractive now that he saw how it was done.

"Next day," Baldwin said, "I got my first taste of skinni'nh sheep.

"See, I's too light for draggi'nh then ol' ewe. I done all right so long's we didn't have to carry 'en, but once we start goi'nh down into the gully to bring 'en up, I plumb give out. Ol' Howie got Little Ringo to help haul carcass, and I got introduce to life in the tunnel."

The sun passed behind a cloud; the breeze abruptly cooled. Baldwin's words overlaid the knife blades' snicking. His voice carried a high-pitched dissonance, something like a grackle or a parrot. *Old Screech* was Ruth's nickname for him. The only time Billy saw them in a room together, the two of them eyed one another like a strange pair of cats.

"Dark like a cave. Dead air. Ten degrees colder'n outside. Sheep pile to one side so wagon can squeeze by. Big Ringo worki'nh one end of pile, Mary worki'nh other end, stove an' water pan in between. Not many hide next to Big Ringo, plenty hide by Mary, so I drag a dead ewe over to Ringo side an' go to skinni'nh. Only one way to stay warm in that tunnel: grab hold and get busy.

"Wasn' long before I wished I'd went the other way. Big Ringo kept up a yack yack yack out the side of his mouth, and it about the nastiest garbage I ever listen to. I could hear better in then days, anyway better'n I do now with these heari'nh aid, but what I heard that day made me wish I couldn'. He talk about fucki'nh sheep an' fucki'nh cattle, how he got too long of a dick an' how a nice heifer felt better'n a whore. Wink at me like I'n the secon'-biggest sheep fucker in the sandhill. I try to preten' like I'n not listni'nh. Didn' know anythin' about fucki'nh no sheep or no whore neither.

"What with all his filthy jabber and me tryi'nh to ignore 'en, I'n getti'nh more sheep skin than Ringo is. Well, Big Ringo pretty stupid, but smart enough to see his tally wasn' goi'nh set good with Howie. He give me a dirty look an' try an' catch up, but work wasn' this fella specialty. By the tine Howie drove wagon in again—Ringo must've heard 'en comi'nh; I didn'—he had three ewe skin to my five. He solve that problem by gatheri'nh up both our hide and throwi'nh 'en on the stack together." Baldwin spat out a fly and wiped his mouth with his wrist. The sun went behind another puffball cloud.

"Door open, let in a blast of snow an' wind. Two Belgian draft horse, eyes half cake shut with ice, come steppi'nh an' blowi'nh an' shaki'nh their harness. Howie standi'nh up in the wagon box, horsehide coat on. Little Ringo close the door behind 'en, an' the tunnel twice as dark as before they come in.

"Howie looki'nh at pile of hide. 'How many you skin?' he ask Big Ringo. 'Fourteen,' says Ringo. 'Kid done five an' I done nine.' He gave me a mean eye. I didn' say nothi'nh.

"'That's good,' ol' Howie says. 'How you get fourteen hide off eight carcass?' Big Ringo forgot the skin carcass layi'nh right there.

"'You calli'nh me a liar?' he says.

"Ol' Howie jus' grin. 'Naw,' he says, 'but I see you ain't good at arithmetic.'"

Baldwin paused in his slicing and stood upright with his hands in the middle of his back. He glanced across at Billy. "I'n getti'nh paid by the day, see, but Ringo an' Mary Lang getti'nh paid by the hide. Howie want to know how many I skin so he don't have to pay Ringo for 'en.

"'You, how many?' Howie says to me, pointi nh a finger. 'Four,' I tell 'en, even though I skin five. 'That soun' right,' Howie says, looki'nh at pile of carcass.

"'Like hell,' Ringo says.

"'He done four, you done four,' Howie says to 'en. 'That's one dollar, an' if you don't like it you can walk.' He take out a piece of chalk an' make a tally on a shingle, an' then he tell Ringo to help his brother unload.

"They throw the woolies off an' throw the skin ones on the wagon—Little Ringo done most of the throwi'nh—an' Howie drive wagon up to Mary Lang pile. Big Ringo follow 'en an' start to argue. 'I get twice as much done,' he says, 'if I didn' have to teach this kid.'

"'Fine,' Howie says. He holler back to me, 'Hey, you. You work on Mary side from now on.'

"When I said I skin four hide, I same as give Ringo twenty-five cent, but now he look like he skin me quick as a sheep. I wasn' sure I wanted to turn my back on 'en. You 'bout to finish over there?'"

Billy watched a western kingbird light on top of a post. The kingbird had caught a bumblebee and was holding it down with one foot, pecking it to death. "I'VE STILL GOT TO DO A BIT MORE ON THIS ONE SIDE."

"I expect your knife is dull. Gi' me."

Billy's back was sore from stooping, and his hand had a cramp from gripping the kitchen knife's slick handle. He unstraddled his heifer and handed the knife to Baldwin. The older man rinsed tallow off it and began his curious sharpening ballet. The shining blade and the dull gray whetstone floated in his hands.

Baldwin took his time to sharpen the two knives. As he continued talking, seated on the tailgate, Billy considered it was part of his job to listen. "Ol' Mary, she a different breed from Ringo. No talk, just slash, rip, slip, another hide on the pile. She use two different skinni'nh knive and sharpen both of 'en after every carcass. While I skin one ewe, she skin four; after that, I just stand an' watch a while. She don't look up or say nothi'nh, but she kind of move aside so I can see what she's doi'nh.

"Pretty soon I drag another ewe over an' go to sharpen my own knife. She stop me. 'Not like that,' she says. 'Le' me show you.' Then she takes my knife and done jus' like I'n doi'nh now, five strokes on one side, turn the knife an' reverse the stone, five strokes on the other. It don't take her but a minute to get my knife sharp, would've took me a half an hour.

"Watchi'nh Mary skin, I see there's an art to it. I forget Big Ringo. Howie an' Little Ringo come an' unload a bunch more ewe; I'n cutti'nh away, doi'nh my best to keep pace, so tire I see spots in front of my eye, when somethi'nh tell me to look up. Big Ringo standi'nh by the water pan an' watchi'nh me an' Mary. Got his knife in one hand an' his peter in the other, an' a grin on his face like he anticipati'nh jacki'nh off. His dick plenty long, all right, but I'n looki'nh at his bad teeth.

"I see a man hold his peter before, so I go back to work. I don't think Mary seen 'en yet. Then I hear a big 'Haw, haw, haw' start up.

"Mary Lang had a deep-voice laugh, you know, kind of like a man? Well, she see Big Ringo dick, an' she cut loose laughi'nh till I could'n help but laugh myself. Ringo turn green like a man swallow chewi'nh tobacco. He cuss us an' show us his knife, but Mary, she don't quit laughi'nh. Finally Ringo took his dick an' his knife an' went back to his end of the tunnel.

"Mary, she glance after 'en an' give me a look. Maybe you know that look; somebody with their back to the wall, scare but rollin' up their sleeve." Baldwin turned his gray eyes to look hard at Billy. "I'n just a kid, seen plenty of fight, but I ain't never seen that look when there's knive in the room."

"SO WHAT HAPPENED?"

"Nothi'nh happen that day," Baldwin said. "Everythi'nh went along about the same."

The day was warming up. Crisp round clouds polkadotted the sky's glass-marble blue. It would have been a good day to drive a car, cruising with the windows down. Billy had heard about a job opening; Turtle Lodge needed a constable. Billy saw himself in uniform, on patrol in a polished black-and-white, revolver at his hip. The kids would stop playing baseball to look at him. Ruth would see him as a man with responsibilities. Flies lit on the bloody knife blade and whirled about his face.

"I see you slowi'nh down over there," Baldwin said. "My wrist getti'nh sore. I work better if I wet my whistle." Billy followed him over to the pickup. Once Baldwin had replaced the whiskey bottle underneath the seat—he offered to share it, but Billy refused—Billy presented his knife, and Baldwin seated himself on the tailgate to sharpen it.

"Next morni'nh," he said, "we all go up to breakfast, an' there Howie wife standi'nh by the door with a busted trunk and a pair of suitcase.

Cookstove cold. 'Harness the horses, Howard,' she says, 'or by ⊂ doi'nh it myself.'

"Howie see his hire hand stari'nh at that bare cookstove with notnɪ'nn on it. He turn all rosy an' chew his mustache. 'All right, Missus,' he says finally, 'I'll take you, only you got to cook these fellas an' Mary breakfast before we go.' Mary standi'nh right there looki'nh at Miz Fredrickson. 'Mary,' Howie says, shameface, 'you can cook dinner for 'en.'

"'I guess I won't,' Mary says. 'I ain't no cook. Ain't no dishwasher neither.'"

Baldwin handed Billy the newer knife and took up the older one. "Howie ol' lady lit up like a Roman candle. She went to cussi'nh Mary, an' I learnt some female language I never thought of. You getti'nh blister?"

"MY WRIST HURTS," Billy admitted. "NO BLISTERS."

"You take this good knife for a while. I believe I'll supervise." Baldwin handed Billy his pet knife along with the newer one. "Use thin blade to cut the hide," he advised, "an' the wide one to peel."

Billy walked to his third dead heifer and stood looking down at her. Baldwin came and stood close by. "Where d'you think?"

"STOMACH?" Billy looked up.

Baldwin nodded. "Don't cut into paunch," he said. "Paunch liquor don't smell nice."

Billy meant to take care, but the thin blade cut like a razor, and when the gasbag popped upward through the slit hide, he touched it. Paunch liquor and gas exploded. "Pee-yooh!" Baldwin whooped, stepping quickly upwind. Billy jumped back, but green slop splattered the leg of his Wranglers.

"SORRY."

"Ne' mind," Baldwin said. "Just silage. Smell won't kill you."

Breathing through thinned lips and working from the upwind side, Billy leaned over the heifer's flank and opened her belly to the anus. Then he leaned above her shoulder and divided the skin over her breastbone and brisket. Once the opening reached her throat, he bypassed her windpipe and severed the esophagus. He and Baldwin then took hold of her and rolled her as far toward her belly as her legs would allow, so that her Technicolor guts slid out. Then they skidded her six feet upwind and rolled her onto her back. Her clean white belly-hair was slimed with bright-green paunch juice. "You go head an' finish 'er," Baldwin said. "You need the practice. The rest is easy." He returned to the tailgate and lit another cigarette.

"Howie sent me an' Jake Mueller to horse barn, spose to hitch 'en up a team for town." Baldwin smoked, and the flies buzzed higher. "Howie had three team, see. But with a foot an' a half of snow on, then horses get use kind of hard. Jake need one team to feed. Howie use one team to haul sheep, an' rest one team. So if Howie take one team to town, we goi'nh be short a team. Weather ain't improve, an' Jake talki'nh to hinself in Dutch. 'Horsus,' he says to me in English. 'Der horsus, dey iss tiret.'

"Big Percheron team, they the best. Next best team Belgian; one bay, one black, old but they got good sense. Last team part Belgian, part rodeo stock. One red roan mare an' one blue roan gelding. Young an' strong, but they waste energy snorti'nh an' danci'nh. Might be a good team in a year or two, but right now, they ain't. Howie got him a saddle horse, too, but his saddle horse ain't use to bein' harness. Only broke to ride.

"Once we got to horse barn, ol' Jake harness that green pair of roan. I help out, don't say nothi'nh. We get 'en hitch, one each side of wagon tongue, which ain't easy with then two knothead kicki'nh an' stompi'nh, an' I open the gate an' Jake drive up to house. Howie hear us comi'nh an' poke his head out. 'God da'nh you, Jake Mueller,' he holler, 'I wanted Bugle an' Blondie!'

"'Dese two restet,' Jake says. 'You vant I go unhitch?'

"Howie look at team an' wagon, then back over his shoulder. 'They be all right,' he says. 'You come in an' get y' breakfast.'"

Billy was faster now at stripping away the hide. He had halfway finished skinning the last heifer. He no longer had to worry about his Wranglers. They were foul and couldn't be made worse.

Baldwin continued. "Fried cornmeal mush an' gravy. Last meal I ever ate in that house, an' it wasn' too God-da'nh pleasant.

"They had 'en a long plank table, kind of like a picnic table, seat about a dozen. Then two Ringo sat down to one end, Howie an' Jake all the way up to other, an' me an' Mary halfway in between. Ol' lady Fredricksen standi'nh up stiff, arm cross, holdi'nh that pancake turner like it was a hammer.

"While we eati'nh, Howie get us all lined out. 'Jake,' he says, 'you be in charge of herd. You can use Bugle an' Blondie on the hayrack. You two Ringo, you ain't much use skinni'nh. Why'n you hitch up Blaze an' Sally an' haul sheep? I pay you both together twenty-fi' cent a carcass; you make about the same as you'd make skinni'nh. Tally hide when I get back, should'nh be no argument. Mary, you do all the skinni'nh. You, kid—' He give me a hard look. 'You ever do any cooki'nh?'

"'No, sir,' I tell 'en. 'I never done hardly any. I seen my ma.'

"Howie chew his mustache a minute. 'You'll learn,' he says. 'You can peel potato, I reckon. Main thing,' he says, 'is to keep the heati'nh stove fire up. This house'll get cold fast if both then stove go out.'

"Next thing, ol' Mary pitch in. 'Why'n you take us all back to town?' she says. 'Then sheep ain't goi'nh nowhere. Wait till the weather warm up.'

"'That's right,' Big Ringo says. 'Settle up with us now. Me an' my brother had enough of this sheep deal.'

"'Let der dead vuns go, Owart,' Jake Mueller says. 'Better ve take care uff dem vot's kicki'nh.'

"'Like hell,' Howie says. His ol' mustache puff out like a cat's tail. 'You all promise me to work two week. No sir. I won't let that money go. By God, I could lose the ranch.'

"Then Howie wife speak up. 'Which would you rather lose, Howard, the ranch or me?'

"'God da'n all of ya!' Howie holler. 'Is everybody here against me? What about you, kid?' he says to me. 'You want to go to town?'" Billy glanced over at his boss. The whiskey bottle had reappeared.

"I'n scared to look at then two Ringo," Baldwin said. "See, I didn' leave nothi'nh in town. Quit school, ma and dad both mad at me. Didn' have no job, didn' have no money, an' I'n too young to get drunk, which is what then two Ringo and Mary got in mind."

"SO WHAT DID YOU TELL HIM?" Billy knelt on the bloody hide and made the final cut. He caught the freed carcass before it slid.

"I told 'en I didn' care. Said I'd stay on an' work if he wanted me." Baldwin tilted the bottle high. It had been half-full earlier.

"'Good for you,' ol' Howie says to me. 'Good for you. Jake, the boy stay. You stay too, right? What about you, Mary?'

"'I ain't ridi'nh in that wagon with *her*,' Howie wife says.

"'Look like you stay, Mary,' Howie says. 'You two sons-a-bitches,' he says to Ringo boy, 'you promise me you'd work two week. By God, you can stay or you can walk. I ain't taki'nh you.'

"'We need fifty cent a carcass,' Big Ringo says, 'or we don't do nothi'nh.'

"'God da'nh ya!' Howie says. 'This war wasn' on, then hide only *worth* fifty cent! I might just as well give you that whole pile of dead sheep.'

"'Don't want no sheep,' Big Ringo says. 'Fifty cent or we don't work.'

"'They get fifty cent, I get fifty cent,' Mary says. 'I ain't afraid to walk to town, neither.'

"'This a God-da'nh holdup,' Howie says. 'I pay thirty-five cent a skin. Thirty-five cent to skinner, thirty-five cent to hauler. An' once this job is over, I hope I never see none of you no more.'" Baldwin belched and tossed the empty bottle into the back of the truck. "Biggest mistake I ever made, openi'nh my mouth that day.

"I went from sheep hauler to skinner to cook. Didn' know nothi'nh about cooki'nh, but I figure I'll stay warm. Howie show me around a bit—ol' lady still guardi'nh the stove—show me trap door over root cellar, coal shed out back, pantry room where a ham an' a side of bacon hangi'nh. All I got to do, he says, is boil potato an' fix a roast, take care of dinner an' supper an' make some kind of breakfast. That's only in case they didn' get back by morni'nh.

"Once he got me lined out, he start planni'nh then Ringo boy day. Howie an' the missus goi'nh take the wagon; Jake Mueller goi'nh need hayrack. Howie an' Jake got thenselve a sled fix up for feedi'nh cottonseed cake, an' he tell Ringo they can use that sled to bring in dead sheep. Sled ain't fancy, just a couple of pole tie together with a platform, but it'll work just as good as a wagon in deep snow. Big Ringo says, yeah, sure, they can handle sled, nothi'nh to it. Howie tell 'en when they get ahead on the hauli'nh, they can help Mary skin.

"'I guess I can keep up with 'en,' Mary says.

"Big Ringo just grin. It the happiest I see 'en look in about three day. Howie catch me listeni'nh an' he says, 'Cook, you better get to washi'nh up in here,' an' I be da'nh if that Ringo didn' jump up an' tie a apron on me an' spin me aroun' till I'n ready to hit 'en.

"When they go out, Ringo boy act like they goi'nh do some work for a change. Pretty soon Howie an' the missus leave for town, an' I'n standi'nh there all alone with a pile of dishes."

Once the carcass had separated from the hide, Billy stood and carried the knives to the truck for washing. "DOESN'T SOUND SO BAD," he said. "WASHING DISHES IN A NICE WARM HOUSE. YOU GOT A PROMOTION."

"Wasn' too bad at first," Baldwin said. "Couple of tine that morni'nh I look out the window an' see Ringo boy whippi'nh that Percheron team up an' down the yard. They holleri'nh, dead sheep falli'nh off both side of sled, but at least they finally showi'nh a little life. I'n thinki'nh 'bout taki'nh coffee out to Mary when I hear then two stompi'nh on the porch. Big Ringo step inside like he own the house; Little Ringo right behind. 'Hey kid,' the little one says. 'Guess what, ol' Howie horse come back.'

"'The hell,' I say. I step to door an' look. Sure enough, there stan' Howie knothead roan team, head over the gate like they just play a big joke on somebody. They still harness together, got the busted wagon tongue hangi'nh between 'en. 'Jeez Christ,' I say, 'look like Howie an' the missus got upset.'

"Then two don't say nothi'nh, and when I look behind me, Big Ringo already over by the stove. I had the cookstove hot, roast in the oven, 'tatas on to boil. Ringo lifti'nh lid off the 'tata pot, an' Little Ringo looki'nh for somethi'nh under the counter.

"'Hey,' I say, 'ain't you even goi'nh to look for 'en?'

"Big Ringo grin. 'You go,' he says. 'We done enough work today. Ol' Mary can skin sheep till Easter.'

"It don't take no genius," Baldwin said, "to see then two ain't goi'nh to budge. What I should of done, I should of gone an' got Mary an' Jake Mueller. Maybe 'tween the three of us we could of whip 'en out of the house."

Billy finished washing the two knives and handed them both to Baldwin. "WHY FIGHT 'EM? LET THE BOSS HANDLE IT."

Baldwin took the two knives and held them upright, studying the blades for chips. "Here the thing," he said. "When I'n getti'nh 'tatas out of the root cellar, I see a gallon crock jug down there, an' I'n monkey enough to find out what was in it. Well, it sure wasn' vinegar. The way Little Ringo goi'nh through then cupboard, I figure he must've smelt my breath." Baldwin put aside the knives. "You can take the log chain out of the back an' throw a couple of half-hitch aroun' that heifer leg."

Billy lifted the chain from the box and tied one end to the rear leg just above the hock. He squatted and hooked the other end to the pickup's frame. "DO YOU SUPPOSE THIS CHAIN IS LONG ENOUGH TO TAKE TWO?"

"We take two next tine," Baldwin said. He glanced at his watch, then up at the sun. It was nearing noon. The heifers were skinned. He didn't seem in a hurry to start another project.

"I put my coat on," Baldwin continued. "In fact, I put on everything I can find, bundle up till I look like Eskimo. Pour a cup of coffee for Mary—then two Ringo take a break from ransacki'nh the place to laugh at me—an' I head out to barn through two feet of snow. I goi'nh out there anyway; have to get some oat to catch Howie knothead team, cause Ringo boy got that good Percheron team wore out.

"Mary act like she about half glad to see me. She glad to see that coffee, anyway. Ringo leave her a big pile of dead sheep, pile of skin ones too; I don't see where they haul any of 'en away. I tell her about Howie team comi'nh back, an' then two Ringo up in the house fixi'nh to get drunk. 'Oh they are, are they,' she says, an' get a thirsty look in her eye. Thank you Howie, I says to myself, for getti'nh me mix up with this crew of booze hound.

"'Maybe you ought to come with me,' I says to Mary. 'I could use some help hitchi'nh that green team.'

"'Got to skin these here sheep,' she says. 'Howie ain't payi'nh me to hitch no horse.'

"I'n thinki'nh she don't get what I'n telli'nh her, so I say it right out. 'I don't like the look of then Ringworm. Maybe you hadn' ought to stay here alone with 'en.'

"She stop sharpeni'nh her skinni'nh knive an' look up. 'Ol' Jake be here,' she says.

"'You think ol' Jake goi'nh help?' I ask her. 'That ol' Dutchman probly get drunk too.'

"'He stout,' she says. Then she look right at me straight. 'Young boy like you,' she says, 'you ain't a da'nh bit safer'n me.'"

Billy recalled two Marines he'd been warned against. There'd been no incidents, but once when his company entered a town, those two had disappeared on business of their own. Nobody said anything about it, and the two of them were back by the time their unit pulled out. Whatever they'd been up to, it only involved Koreans. There'd been no complaints. BALDWIN CLIMBED BEHIND the steering wheel and started the engine. Billy got in on the passenger side and watched behind them as the log chain tightened and the carcass slipped from the hide. The paunch burst open and slopped itself empty, and somewhere in the middle of the pasture the string of guts caught on a soapweed and broke off. The nude and empty carcass bumped and twisted, scuffing from slick yellow-pink to brick-red where the tallow had been scraped away.

Baldwin headed the pickup toward the corner of the pasture farthest from the house. He steered a wide arc to the edge of a pocket where a scatter of animal bones lay on windblown sand, along with a few broken posts and a roll of rusted sheep fence. A badger had dug out a den under the three-foot bank. "Then badger goi'nh have thenselves a picnic," Baldwin said as he stopped the truck. "I ought to poison the sons-a-bitches."

Billy stood on the chain to get the tightness out of it, then unhooked it from the truck frame and untied the heifer's leg. Baldwin grabbed the heifer's ears, Billy took hold of the tail, and together they slid the carcass over the edge. "Starti'nh to stink already," Baldwin said.

"THE COYOTES WILL BE SINGING OUT HERE TONIGHT." Billy threw the chain into the box and hopped in the cab. Baldwin put the idling truck in gear. His bleached-out eyes flicked over the pasture as they left the blowout.

"Took me a good half hour to get then Percheron fed an' put away. Ringo boy had 'en all played out, nobody goi'nh take care of 'en if I don't. I catch Jake Mueller out to horse barn, but when I try an' tell him what been goi'nh on, ol' Jake smell my whiskey breath too. Jake pull his turnip watch out. 'Watch says noon, time to eat,' he says. Don't nobody get between a Dutchman and his dinner. Or his liquor.

"I see I'n on my own. I'd lef' then two knothead roan tied to Miz Fredricksen fence. I go back an' give 'en some oat and get 'en hitch to Howie sled. Then I go to house an' wrap a couple 'tatas in a dishtowel. Jake Mueller an' both Ringo sitti'nh all buddy-buddy, roast on table, jug on floor. Mary not in from skinni'nh yet. I go back out in cold, get on Howie cake sled, slap the rein. Then two knothead roan give a jump, an' now all I got tine to worry 'bout is just to stay on top of sled.

"By this tine the sun come out bright. Wasn' snowi'nh to mount to anythi'nh. Da'nh cold, though. I can follow Howie wagon track, no trouble, but I wasn' happy bei'nh out there by mysell. Snow on the ground, wind come up, you can get lost quick in the sandhill. People done it before, got lost and died just tryi'nh to find the outhouse." They approached the swale with the dead heifers, and Baldwin swung the pickup wide to pull up alongside. Billy jumped out to lift the chain over the side of the box.

The rear bumper on Baldwin's pickup had been replaced by an angle-iron with a hole for a clevis. Billy tied one end of the chain around the nearest heifer's leg and pulled the loose end through the gap. There wasn't enough chain to reach the next carcass, but they both took hold, Billy pulling and Baldwin pushing, and skidded the second heifer closer to the truck. Billy tied her on and found a piece of baling wire to secure the chain, and Baldwin got behind the steering wheel again and they drove off, slower this time. When Billy looked back, the pink carcasses had slid together and were nudging each other like teenagers on their way to a makeout party.

"I come to Howie wagon in about two mile," Baldwin said. "Wagon hadn' been upset, just standi'nh empty in a snowdrift with the tongue broke off. I follow Howie an' Miz Fredricksen track toward a neighbor place a half-mile farther on, an' when I top the hill I see smoke comi'nh fron the chimney.

"So, I drive on in, figure I'll get me somethi'nh else to eat beside then two cold 'tatas I been carryi'nh. I'n thinki'nh maybe I should of brought extra team an' a piece of wood an' tool to fix the wagon tongue; maybe Howie goi'nh give me hell because I didn'. But I'n so disgusted with the whole da'nh crew by then, I didn' care if he give me hell, so long's I get warm."

"SOUNDS LIKE ONE OF THOSE DAYS." A crow flew up from the direction of the blowout and flapped toward a distant grove, rowing the air above the hills. A length of yellow intestine dangled from its claws.

"One o' those day, all right. Say, you heard this before?" Billy shrugged. After a pause to study him, Baldwin went on. "I tie up horses to the gatepost, an' neighbor wife come an' let me in the front door. Now, what you spose Howie an' the missus doi'nh?"

"I DON'T KNOW," Billy said. "POPPING POPCORN?"

"Sitti'nh at the pyanna bench, lovey as a couple parakeet," Baldwin said. "Missus picki'nh out a tune an' Howie singi'nh. Neighbor husban'—Douglas is the name—sitti'nh by the stove in his stocki'nh feet, an' his wife pouri'nh cider. I went an' harness then knothead roan, come all this way, find 'en havi'nh thenselve a singalong.

"Howie wife says, 'It's one of those bad men, Howard.'

"Ol' Howie look aroun'. 'Hell, it's the kid,' he says. 'What *you* doi'nh here? I thought I give you order to mind the cookstove.'

"'Horse come back,' I say. 'I wanted to fine out if you was froze to death.'

"'Well,' he says, 'we ain't.' Then both of 'en turn back to the pyanna, an' I decide that once I get warm up I'n goi'nh walk to town. But then Miz Douglas—same age Miz Fredricksen, only nicer—tell me to take my coat off. She give me cocoa an' a fresh-bake roll, an' fuss over me like I ain't had nobody do in a while. By the tine Howie an' Miz Fredricksen done with the pyanna, I ain't in no hurry to leave. I even ask for some cider."

Two more crows flew up from the blowout. Baldwin didn't drive the truck as close to the edge this time. The chained carcasses slid apart as he made the turn. "IF YOU'D BACK IT UP A FOOT, THEY'D BE EASIER TO UNHOOK," Billy said, but Baldwin was already getting out of the truck. Billy got down also and yanked at one of the carcasses to put slack in the chain. He unhitched both carcasses and dumped the chain back in the pickup box, and Baldwin helped him roll the nearest heifer over the rim. They turned back to look at the second heifer, slightly downhill from the lip and seven or eight feet away. "I'LL HOOK HER ON AND YOU CAN SWING AROUND AGAIN."

"Nah," Baldwin said. "Grab ahold."

Baldwin caught hold of the heifer's tail, and Billy took her ears. His purchase was poor; Baldwin dragged her hind end closer to the blowout, but Billy kept losing his grip. He tried grasping the carcass by the nose and lower jaw; finally, he wrapped his arms around the unskinned head, rubbing his shirtsleeve into the meat of the neck. Baldwin grunted and gave the tail a sudden heave; the corpse fell away and twisted, and Billy lost his balance. He caught himself at the edge of the blowout, hands braced on crumbling sand, staring straight down at the animal's bulging eyeball. The heifer's cornea had glazed over and her pupil was turning from black to soapy blue; the dark veins around the iris formed a net. Billy panicked, fighting gravity to scramble backward as sand slid into the heifer's unblinking eye.

A strong hand grabbed his belt and pulled him back. Billy sprang to his feet. "Well, that one way to do it," Baldwin said as he gripped Billy's elbow. "You all right?"

Billy took a couple of deep breaths and shook his head to clear it. "I'LL BE FINE. JUST GIVE ME A MINUTE."

"It turn out," Baldwin said, once they were back inside the cab—Billy's heart rate was returning to normal—"Howie wife hasn' been off the place in about three month. Howie says, by God, they goi'nh see a picture show, an' the God-da'nh bank can have the God-da'nh ranch, an' he doesn' care if then God-da'nh sheep all starve, and that God-da'nh Jake can starve with 'en. Douglas own a Model T that'll run, an' the road past their place open. Howie says Douglas figure they can all four get to town.

"I'n jus' a kid, but I let 'en know I didn' like that plan. 'What about the rest of us?' I ask 'en. 'What you spect me an' Mary to do? Then Ringo foun' your liquor, ain't goi'nh skin no sheep. Be lucky if you still got a house by the tine you get back.'

"Ol' Howie flew mad an' holler at me. 'You go back an' cook for 'en like you spose to! Fucki'nh hire men worse'n then God-da'nh fucki'nh sheep, can't leave 'en alone five minute! My sweetheart want to see a picture show, an' by God I'n goi'nh take her, an' the rest of you can fucki'nh go to hell!'

"I take a good look at his missus, an' I see she about to cry, and I see ol' Howie kind of got his hands full there.

"Miz Douglas gi' me somethi'nh to eat, an' I use Howie team to help drag Douglas Model T out to road. All this take a while, mus' be four, four-thirty when I start back for Fredricksen place. Getti'nh dark by tine I drive into the yard. Firs' thing I see, house window dark, no lantern lit, no chimney smoke an' house door standi'nh open."

Billy shivered, though June sunlight fell on his lap. He could still feel the dead heifer's pupil drawing him down. "HOW COLD WAS IT?"

"Didn' see no thermometer.

"Team an' sled make plenty of noise, so I go straight up to door, don't bother sneaki'nh. I even stomp snow off my boot, let 'en know I'n comi'nh. Dark inside, can't see nothi'nh, but I think maybe I hear snori'nh, so I go back out an' pull the door shut so whoever pass out in there won't freeze to death. Then I go to put team away. I didn' take tine to curry 'en, but I did give 'en hay an' oat. Belgian team in the barn, ol' Percheron team where I left 'en. Didn' see no sign of Jake Mueller, so I fed both then other team, too. Look like I got to do everybody else work aroun' there."

They approached the swale with the hides and the remaining carcasses. Billy thought about the dead heifer and tried to imagine a lifetime of chewing grass. "WEREN'T YOU SUPPOSED TO BE THE COOK? I WOULD'VE JUST STAYED IN THE HOUSE."

"Not with then two Ringo, you wouldn'," Baldwin said. "I didn' trust 'en sober, an' they been drinki'nh all afternoon.

"Anyhow, plumb dark before I went to sheep barn to check on Mary." Baldwin backed the pickup near the remaining two carcasses, and Billy got out and chained their legs to the back of the truck. Baldwin then drove ahead a few feet, jerking the flayed carcasses off their hides, and shut off the motor. "This the hard part," he said, swinging the truck door open. "Heavy lifti'nh." He stooped over one of the hides and folded the leg-skin inward. "You goi'nh just stan' there?"

Billy helped fold each of the hides into a package three feet square. It took the two of them to lift each package into the truck. "Tell you what heavy," Baldwin said. "Ol' horsehide overcoat heavy. Take a good man just to stan' up in 'en."

"WHAT DID YOU WEAR TO KEEP WARM BACK THEN?"

"Sheepskin jacket," Baldwin said. "Sears wool pant. Scotch cap. Wool underwear, kep' 'en on all winter. Itch to drive you crazy." The truck sat lower from the weight of the five hides; they got back in, Baldwin gunned the engine, and the final two carcasses bumped behind them at the ends of the chain.

Baldwin lit a cigarette. "I spose you heard all this at the coffee shop," he said. "That's all right; just let 'en talk. Nobody still alive who seen it. Nobody but me an' Mary.

"Dark in sheep barn, darker in alley. First body I trip over is Jake Mueller. I think he's a sheep carcass till I feel his mustache. Next I find Mary, over by the stove; she naked an' cold, but breathi'nh. I put my coat over her an' hunt till I found a lantern. Once I get it lit, I can see she in bad shape, bloody at both end, goi'nh die right there unless I do somethi'nh. Didn' dare take her to the house or bunkhouse either. Didn' want then Ringo to even know I'n on the place.

"I did what any kid would've done," Baldwin said. "I panic. Walk in circle, talk to mysell. After I get some sense back, I make a bed out of hay bale an' sheep hide. When I drag Mary up onto it, she cuss me, so I know she probly goi'nh live.

"I put my coat back on an' cover Mary up with sheep hide. Then hide ain't been shear since summer, got wool on 'en four inch thick. Then I see that little kerosene stove still goi'nh. Don't put out no heat to speak of, but— You 'member they left a pan on stove, melt snow for sharpeni'nh knive? Blood and sheep fat in it, not too clean, but I'n hungry enough to think it smell like soup. I'n wishi'nh I had some of Howie whiskey to warm us up, but that sheep broth be better'n nothi'nh. I found Mary coffee cup an' dip it in.

"That cup of sheep broth save ol' Mary life. She's had forty year to thank me, but she never done it." Baldwin glanced at Billy. "Think I should've gone for sheriff? She'd been froze by the tine I got back. If then Ringo didn' sober up an' rape her some more.

"Fifteen, an' I never seen a woman naked." They arrived at the rim of the blowout. Two crows and a magpie flew up. Baldwin glanced at his wristwatch. The sun, now vertical, was already blackening the carcasses. The magpies had pecked dark red holes into the meat.

"I found skinni'nh knife an' sat there holdi'nh it, thinki'nh then two Ringo goi'nh come for me any minute. Cold, hungry, worn-out tire an' scare to death. Mary says to me, 'I think somethi'nh happen to Jake.' I didn' say nothi'nh. Next thing she says, 'This wool itchi'nh me like blazes. You find me my shirt an' overall an' step away.'

"When I come back, she layi'nh like before, excep' she got one hide over her 'stead of three. 'You better ride an' get the sheriff,' she says. 'Tell 'en if there ain't been a murder yet, there goi'nh be one.'

"'Mary, you ain't got no chance agains' then two,' I say. 'If I go to town, you ought to come with me.'

"'Can't ride,' she says. 'Too sore. You see any knive aroun' here?'

"'I'n carryi'nh one,' I say, an' show it to her.

"'I recollect that one dull,' she says. 'Whet it for me.' She close her eyes. Can't tell if she asleep or awake, but I sharpen the knife. Done a good job, too. I done it just like she taught me." Baldwin finished his cigarette and stubbed it out. "Unhook then yearli'nh an' we go get ourselve some dinner."

"I HEARD THE MARY LANG SAGA IN TOWN," Billy said. "I DIDN'T KNOW YOU WERE IN IT."

"I'n in it, all right. Wish I hadn' been.

"I sharpen the knife, an' Mary hold out her hand from under the sheepskin. 'Take Howie saddle horse,' she says to me. 'That way, then bastard can't catch up with you. An' blow out the lantern 'fore you go. I rest better in the dark.'

"I left her with two knive beside her an' run for the horse barn. I see a yellow window up at the house; somebody in there sober enough to light a lamp. I'n tryi'nh to go quiet, but I'n maki'nh a noise like a elephant on that squeaki'nh snow.

"Horse barn darker'n seventy-nine black cat, but I ain't about to light no lantern or strike no match. Take tine to find bridle an' blanket for Howie saddle horse. Once I find 'en, got to locate horse. I carry tackle over to stall where I think saddle horse is at, an' when horse come up to sniff me I quick put bridle on, even though I kind of notice it's too tight. Lead 'en out into alley to saddle up. Cinch don't fit good either, an' that da'nh horse shuffle an' fuss an' try to kick me."

"YOU GOT HOLD OF ONE OF THOSE GREEN WORK HORSES INSTEAD OF THE SADDLE HORSE."

"That's right." Baldwin stood behind Billy and watched him unchain the carcasses. Together they tipped one and then the other one over the bank; Billy kept away from the edge and avoided looking down. As he took sand to scrub the tallow off his hands, some important thing left unfinished tugged at his mind.

"It was one of them knothead roan." Baldwin walked to his side of the pickup and twisted the door handle. "I no more'n get the cinch let out when the door swing open an' I see Big Ringo outline against the snow. Wobbly on his feet, but walki'nh. 'Jake?' he says. 'That you, Jake?' I don't feel like I need to remind 'en he kill Jake already. Then I see 'en hunti'nh through his pocket for a match.

"I figure I'n dead anyhow, so I pull the cinch tight, jump up an' acrost the saddle, swing my leg around, an' give that big young roan a kick an' a yell. I'n layi'nh flat down over saddle horn, face in mane, an' that big roan horse just run right over Ringo. I never know if he step on 'en or not. What's the matter with you? You look like you swallow a toad."

"MY KNIFE CASE IS EMPTY. MY BAYONET IS GONE."

"The hell. Well, you can come back an' look for it after dinner."

"NOT AFTER DINNER! WE HAVE TO FIND IT NOW! GO BACK TO WHERE WE WERE. YOU THREW IT AT THE TRUCK, REMEMBER?"

"I'n hungry. You ain't goi'nh find it—"

"GOD *DAMN* IT!" Billy pulled open the passenger door and got out and slammed it shut. The rolled-down glass rattled in its channel. "THAT BAYONET IS IMPORTANT TO ME! I BROUGHT IT FROM KOREA!" He turned to follow the track of wheel-bent grass. The swale was a half-mile back across the pasture, but Billy did not fear walking. He'd retreated on foot half the length of the Korean peninsula, with bullets and shrapnel zipping past him along the way.

He heard the pickup's engine start. The truck came purring and rattling up alongside him. "Get in," Baldwin said. "I take you."

"FUCK YOU!" Billy screamed to make himself understood. "YOU THREW MY BAYONET AND LOST IT!" He stomped the heels of his boots into sandhills sod no thicker than a dead man's skin.

The truck creaked along beside him at a walking pace. "Calm down," Baldwin said. "I goi'nh make sure you find it. That big roan horse, he buck off 'cross the yard—"

"SHUT UP!" Billy yelled. "I HEARD IT! YOU RODE TO TOWN AND STAYED ALL NIGHT WITH THE SHERIFF! YOU WENT OUT WITH SOME MEN IN THE MORNING! SHE'D KILLED THEM BOTH AND SKINNED THEM AND NAILED THE SKINS UP ON THE WALL! SHE EVEN SKINNED OUT THEIR DICKS!"

"She only skin Big Ringo. Little Ringo walk off into snow. Found 'en next spring."

"I DON'T CARE."

"Hanh?"

"I SAID, FUCK YOU! I QUIT! I DON'T CARE ONE RAT'S-ASS TOOT ABOUT THOSE RINGOS, OR HOWIE FREDERICKSEN, OR COWS, OR SHEEP, OR YOU OR YOUR GOD-DAMNED RANCH—"

"Perfect hide, no hole anywhere. Couldn' even see how she kill 'en." They continued along in silence. "No need to quit," Baldwin said. "I goi'nh fire you anyway. You ain't worth shit as a hire hand."

IT TOOK THEM an hour to find the bayonet. Billy had given up looking when Baldwin spotted the pommel sticking out of the sand where the pickup's wheel had run over it. He pulled it up like a root and handed it over. "Blade bent," he said. "Too bad."

"YEAH, WELL," Billy said. "IT DIDN'T COST ME ANYTHING BESIDES A YEAR OF MY LIFE, GETTING SHOT AT AND FREEZING MY ASS."

"You sure you want to keep it? Goi'nh be tough to straighten. If I heat it, probly take the temper out."

"I'LL KEEP IT." One wooden grip-half was split away and gone. The other half hung loosely on its rivet.

"Come on up to the house," Baldwin said. "I write you out a check after dinner." He fished in his pocket and brought up a ring of keys. A pewter medal, its face worn smooth, dangled on the ring. "Know what this is?"

"IT'S A SAINT CHRISTOPHER'S MEDAL. I SAW THEM IN KOREA."

"Saint Christopher medal," Baldwin said. "My wife Catholic. Use to be. She says it spose to give 'en protection."

"SO WHERE'D YOU GET IT?"

"I took it off of Ringo. We found his body skin an' naked in the sheep barn, standi'nh up and wire to a post. Guess he come back for some more of Mary an' got more'n he wanted." Baldwin turned the medal over. "Use to have a silver chain on, but it broke. Ol' Mary must've taken it off to skin 'en, then put it back around his neck. Had it on when we found 'en."

"WHY WOULD HE WANT PROTECTION, A MAN LIKE HIM?"

"I wouldn' know. Protection from hinself, maybe. I carry it ever since. I ain't too good of a person, but I ain't as bad as I might be." Baldwin started taking the medal off the key ring. "I give it to you cause I ruin your bayonet."

"YOU KEEP IT," Billy said. "IT CAME TO YOU. THE BAYONET CAME TO ME."

"You sure?" Baldwin glanced at the bent blade.

"YOU KEEP IT. I SPOILED YOUR STORY. I APOLOGIZE."

Baldwin thumbed the smooth face of the medal. "Sometine I feel bad I took it off 'en. Should of let 'en bury 'en with it, since he didn' have no skin."

"THEY DIDN'T BURY HIS SKIN WITH HIM?"

"I guess somebody must've took it." Baldwin looked down and pocketed the medal. "Let's go an' get ourselve some dinner. This bottle empty. I got me another one in the Frigidaire."

EVERY TOWN HAS its Bloody Mary, a story told around the campfire by twelve-year-olds to frighten one another. Baldwin's yarn meant no more than that to Billy, until the dispatcher sent him to the Sailors of Galilee Nursing Home to transport a patient (he had a different job by then). He drove up in his patrol car to find a white-haired woman in a wheelchair, with two of the nursing-home staff keeping a safe distance. "She needs to go in for X-rays," one of them said. "She's had a fall."

"What happened?"

"She tried to get the server with a butter knife." The woman in the wheelchair said nothing. Her toothless jaw was working and her eyes looked teary.

"I'll take care of it," Billy said. "Can she stand up and slide onto the car seat?"

"You might have to help her," the attendant said. "Watch yourself."

"No problems," Billy said. He took the patient's elbow. "Come, grandma," he said. "We're going for a ride."

"Don't 'grandma' me," the white-haired woman said. "I ain't never had no husband, and I don't want none."

"OK, you're not a grandma," Billy said. "Help me get you in the car."

"I was rape once," the old woman said. "I fixed him, though."

"This is our own Bloody Mary," the attendant said. "Local legend. The real deal."

Bloody Mary was barely mobile, a menace no longer. Her large head thrust itself forward and jiggled on its stem. The texture of her arm when he assisted her was that of an overripe tomato. From the freckles that had spread and grown together, he could guess that she'd once been a redhead. He slid her onto the seat without trouble, though her weight sagged the car.

"I hear you're a famous man-killer," he said once they were moving. "I'm proud to meet you."

"I see you carry a gun," she said in reply. "Ever use it?"

"Machine-gunner, United States Marine Corps," Billy said. "They didn't ship me all the way to Korea to shoot rocks and trees."

"Killin' a man ain't edifying. Too easy. I wisht I had me some ice cream."

They were approaching the Dairy Princess at the turnoff to the hospital. Billy wheeled the black-and-white patrol car into one of the stalls. He studied Mary from the corner of his eye as he waited for the girl to come out.

The carhop bent toward the window. Her uniform collar was buttoned. "What do you want?"

"Two soft serves. Small. Vanilla."

"I can't eat no ice cream," Mary said. "I got diabetes."

"One small cone won't hurt. Do you know Baldwin McDonough?"

"I known him since he was a boy. He's a hard worker who would rather of been useless. You don't never want to play no cards with Baldwin. He will skin you."

"That's a funny choice of language."

"Not to me, it ain't. Are you tryin' to arrest me? I'm done talkin' to you."

Mary ate the soft ice cream in silence, and he delivered her to the hospital. They met him on the ambulance apron with a wheelchair. Before he came around to help her out of the car, she said, "I guess you want to know where his skin is at. That's the thing they all say to me: 'What did you do with the skin?'"

"I wasn't going to ask," Billy said. "You're not under investigation."

"I never had it. Somebody else took it. It's over to the Elks Club, rolled up in a cardboard tube." Mary twisted her old neck sidewise and gave him a slow wink. "You can tell 'em I sent you," she said.

The Law

ONE BRIGHT OCTOBER Sunday in 1952, Billy Dixon sat on his own front step, enjoying the Nebraska sunshine and working on the Russian bayonet he'd brought home from the war. He'd repositioned the blade of a hacksaw and was cutting away the rivets of the broken grip when his neighbor, Gerard Horse Looking, came over to watch. Gerard Horse Looking was an enormous Lakota Indian, Billy's age or a little younger, who lived next door in a 35-foot trailer. "Hey, brother," he said. "Pretty day, enit? Would you happen to have a beer?"

Billy did not drink regularly, and, as a member of the law-enforcement profession, he did not think providing alcohol to an Indian was a misdemeanor he wanted to commit. "I don't," he said, "but I can put a pot of coffee on."

"Coffee's good, coffee's good," the other said. "I like plenty of sugar."

Gerard Horse Looking was not talkative, and Billy was inclined to be reticent with a man he might be called upon to arrest. Nevertheless it felt good to sit with somebody. His new life as a small-town cop tended to be lonely. "How are you doing?" he asked Gerard. "I hear you got a job with the railroad."

"Ah, they fired me," Gerard Horse Looking replied. "They said I took too many days off. Did you know I had a sister?"

"No, I did not know that about you."

"She's coming to live with me," Gerard Horse Looking said. "I was wondering if you could keep an eye on her sometimes."

"That depends. How old is she?"

"I dunno. Eleven, maybe."

Bernadette Horse Looking turned out to be twelve, though she had the scrawny body of a ten-year-old. She hated Billy right from the beginning. Gerard and Bernadette kept noisy house like a pair of magpies. Gerard insisted that Bernadette attend school, though he hadn't gone much himself, and their fights continued long after the first-period bell. Billy had night duty, so he hoped they would let him sleep; he could hardly call the day constable if they woke him. If he showed his face to complain, Gerard would ask him to drive the little hellcat to the door of the school. The only way to make sure she went in was to walk her inside.

Billy's job as night constable in the town of Turtle Lodge consisted mostly of putting Indians in jail. He became familiar with blood, vomit, fecal matter, urine, and sperm. The latter he encountered on the bars of jail cells, more often than anyone would expect. He learned right away which drunken teenagers to arrest and which to carry home to their mothers. He learned that the judge's wife shoplifted; the judge always paid for her thefts, and the town merchants did not think of it as a problem. Habitual drunks who were white were not to be bothered unless they drove too dangerously. Two illegal poker games went on in the town, one for businessmen and cattlemen who indulged, the other for cowboys and mechanics. Billy was entitled to a rakeoff from the second if he let the first alone. Bootlegging into the nearby Indian reservation was done openly, and he was cautioned not to talk with FBI agents, who bore the task of enforcement on the South Dakota end. They wore sunglasses and dark-gray suits with concealed holsters, and passed through the town of Turtle Lodge like movie stars.

The woman who walked the streets in furs and with a monkey on her shoulder was the wife of a millionaire rancher. No whorehouse currently operated in Turtle Lodge, Nebraska.

Billy hoped that his uniform would impress his pretty cousin, but Ruth seemed to have regard only for money. A constable didn't earn much of that. Billy had applied to be deputy sheriff under Starchy Sedgwick, but the sheriff said he wasn't old enough and that a deputy sheriff ought at least to be able to grow a decent mustache. Rudy McDonough put in a word at City Hall and got him the constable job. There were two, Day Constable and Night Constable, and the nighttime cop had needed to be let go. He couldn't do the work of lifting drunks up off the sidewalk, and his hands had become too shaky to unlock handcuffs.

Billy bought a square little run-down house in a neighborhood south of the railroad tracks and spent most of his off-hours fixing it. For a young man of good looks and energy, whose mere presence in a bar destroyed all conversation, there was little that was entertaining to do. His relatives the McDonoughs had helped him find employment, but they didn't invite him to supper. "I could have been killed in Korea," he counseled himself. "Yet I have lived to become an important person, and I own a house." He might have added, in an unimportant town.

The city clerk could marry couples and levy fines up to fifteen dollars, but most cases went before Judge Abe Brown, who ruled the top floor of the county courthouse. Billy was always glad to testify before Judge Brown because he could pass by the treasurer's office where his cousin Ruth worked. Ruth had been a skinny beanpole in the back seat of her Model T; now she was as lithe a package of sex as a man could desire. Wearing flats or low wedge heels, slim legs encased in black or navy pants, she strode the hallways of the courthouse with a mannish assurance, trailing cigarette smoke that was part of her allure. Ruth's husband was away on the road as his trucking business required, but nothing Billy said to her gained him access. Ruth's sister, Ellen McDonough, disliked Billy, even though she had helped him relocate. Ellen taught in the Turtle Lodge high school, and whenever Billy spoke to her, he felt he had to be careful with his grammar.

Things went on like this for a couple of years. The only change was that Ruth and Bernadette got older, and Billy felt his morals begin to loosen. Mrs. Althea Dodson, wife of the town's pharmacist, called in for him to get her cat down from a tree. When he'd arrived, the cat was eating salmon from a dish on the kitchen counter. She then asked him to investigate a gas leak in the basement, and when he'd turned around, there she was naked, with her great breasts resting more than halfway to her navel. Though her cat was out of danger, he had sprung straight to the rescue, and done her service as befit an ex-Marine.

Wendy Kugelman, originally from Berlin, once a war bride, now divorced, called in to ask for someone to come and see about a prowler (she was terrified of her ex-husband, who lived elsewhere but sometimes passed through on one of his rants). She had taken Billy to the garden to show where the man had stood. There was a clear view of her bedroom window, and when she thought of herself undressed, she'd gone weak in the knees. Billy helped her to a trellised bench, where her weakness became inviting.

There were more of these 45-minute investigations, but Billy was careful to not let himself be expected. To preserve his looks and stamina, he watched what he ate, and, when the squabbling Horse Lookings let him have a morning's sleep, he ran his three miles a day, out to Baxter's Pond and back. He shot pheasants in the fall and took part in the rattlesnake hunt up on Turtle Lodge Butte. In short, he lived within the normal pattern of a small-town cop. Always recognized and always a stranger, he knew the lives of the local saints better than the saints themselves.

BILLY LEARNED ABOUT his cousin's paramour by accident. She drove a shiny two-tone Chevy Bel Air, and she often parked it at noon in front of the Pendergast Hotel. One lunch hour, feeling desperate, he had entered the hotel's restaurant in hope of seeing her. Ruth was not in evidence, though her car was parked outside. He ordered soup and a sandwich and took a table where he could watch the lobby. Sure enough, she passed through at five minutes until one o'clock. After she drove away, a man Billy recognized as the county tax assessor came into the restaurant and ordered coffee and a slice of pie. He was darkly handsome, with a full head of curly black hair, and there was nothing about him to indicate that he'd been up to anything. Nevertheless, Billy understood what had taken place. He'd been so shocked that he'd left without paying. When he came to his senses and returned with two dollars, he was told the assessor had picked up his check.

"I hear you've been spying on me," was all Ruth had to say about it. "Keep it up. It will contribute to your education." Billy felt more heartbroken at the age of twenty-three than he'd felt at thirteen when he'd heard she was married.

Heartbroken or not, he still had his constable job. He took what she said as a kind of permission and memorized the license plate of every vehicle in town, so that he knew who went where during his shift and at other times. He knew when somebody's car was out of place, and he learned by this means that the tax assessor, whom he viewed as his enemy, visited a house where lived the grass widow of a seller of Oldsmobiles. By watching this driveway in turn, Billy learned that his other cousin, Ellen McDonough, had a husband who sometimes cheated on her. And so on. Ruth's lawful spouse, a trucker named George Smith, did not show up on Billy's license-plate radar, but their ten-year-old was prone to slipping out at night, peeping in windows and setting trash can fires. Billy could have caught him a time or two, but he preferred to wait until he did something more serious.

Ruth Smith—that was her name now—filled her prescriptions at both of Turtle Lodge's pharmacies. That failed to strike Billy as odd until he learned that she'd gotten a speeding ticket in one of the neighboring counties. She'd told the arresting officer that she had to get to that other town's drug store before it closed.

Then there was the matter of Bernadette Horse Looking.

Dunlap County's social structure had layers, and the bottom layer was scruffy. Broken cowboys unable to ride and work cattle lived in rooms above bars and hair salons, helping out with the livestock auction for pocket money. Hard-luck ranchers subsisted on deer meat and chewing tobacco, paying their notes to the bank in the fall when they sold their steers. Both types of men found their women among the Indians, whom they preyed upon with liquor.

It was the daytime constable, Jonesey, who caught Florian Hoffer in a room above the feed store, plying an underage Indian girl with sloe gin. Florian owned a flat-roofed shack on a grazed-off section of sandhills. People figured he might be sixty, since his overalls looked to be forty-five. He was poorly shaven and smelled of ancient sweat and horse liniment, and he spoke ungrammatical English with an accent. Had the young girl been Caucasian, Florian Hoffer would have gone to prison. As it was, he paid a fine of twenty dollars and went home in time to milk his cows. Billy Dixon, even though he was technically off duty, got called in to take the fourteen-year-old to try and find her brother.

The underage Indian girl was Bernadette.

"Behave yourself," he said as he shoved her into his car (the town's patrol car was still in use by the astute Jonesey). "I don't want to have to put you in handcuffs."

"Just try it, mister Snake Hips," she replied. "I'll make you sorry."

Gerard Horse Looking did not answer Billy's knock at their trailer. "Any ideas?" he asked the girl. "I can't just turn you loose. You might start more trouble."

"In this town? That's a laugh," she said. "How should I know where my brother is? He's a grownup. You're a grownup. Figure it out."

In her body Bernadette resembled a child, with only a hint of broadening here and there, but her face was full and alive, with black upslanted eyes and pouty lips. "You ought to fix your hair," Billy told her. "You look like somebody dipped a porcupine in road tar."

"Let me go inside and get my comb."

"You'll lock the door on me."

"It doesn't lock. You can come in with me."

Billy had lived next door for more than a year, but he had never been inside their trailer. The front door opened onto a wreckage of cereal boxes, Velveeta wrappers, and broken furniture. One window that would have looked toward the street was blocked with cardboard. The doors hung crookedly off the cabinets, and the refrigerator stood dark and empty. There was no response from the light switch. Billy knew that the Horse Lookings used an outhouse at the back of their lot, but he hadn't thought about the way of living that implied. They took their drinking water from an outdoor faucet at the side of his house.

"Where do you wash dishes?" he asked her, looking around. The kitchen sink was piled with rolled-up newspapers. "Where do you take baths?"

"We mostly eat out of the packages," she said. "We take baths in the river."

"You mean in Baxter's Creek," Billy said. "The river is thirteen miles."

Bernadette went to the rear of the trailer to look for a comb. The ceiling was so low that Billy felt the need to stoop, though the top of his head did not touch. There was no place to sit and nothing to read, and anyway the light was poor. "What are you doing back there?" he called out after a time. "We need to go look for your brother."

"My brother's all right," she called back. "He takes care of himself."

"It's not Gerard that I'm worried about. I need to get rid of you. I'm supposed to go on duty." Billy glanced out through a gap in the window. Except for his personal car, the street was empty.

"Come on back here for a minute. I won't bite you."

Billy made his way down a cramped corridor, past a narrow bathroom jammed with clothes and cardboard boxes. The bedroom at the rear was empty. Turning back, he saw a door that he'd missed and pulled it open. In a room hardly big enough for a dog to turn around in, the girl lay on a mattress on the floor, with her feet up, playing with her toes. She wore not a stitch. "What about it, cop boy," she said, frowning up at him. "Do those tin pants come off?"

Billy got to work five minutes late that afternoon. The odious Jonesey smirked when he handed over the keys.

Billy went off duty at two., one hour after the bars closed. Bernadette was waiting. That night the girl wouldn't leave him; they made love at Billy's after she'd had a bath. She clung in her sleep like a monkey, and when he woke at sunrise he wanted sex again and again until his nuts ached and he felt a strong need to pee. Then, when he went into the bathroom and raised the lid, he couldn't. When he came back to bed, she was available, and when he still hadn't peed and it was getting near four p.m., Billy sent the girl home and called the hospital. The urge to urinate was agonizing, even though he could barely make a drip, and to his shame he had to be catheterized. He was given a prescription for sulfadiazine, and when he went to fill it, there was Ruth, collecting a bottle of black-and-yellow pills.

"Good afternoon," Billy said, shamefaced.

"Good evening," his cousin replied. "What's the matter with you? Aren't you supposed to be on duty?"

"They tell me I've got a bladder infection. What about you?"

"These are nothing," Ruth said. "I take them for my nerves. When are you coming over?"

"I don't know," Billy said. "Your husband doesn't like me."

"We'll have you over for dinner one of these days," she said. "I don't care too much what old George likes."

They left the pharmacy together. He watched her walk away, wondering when she'd started saying "dinner" when she meant "supper."

Billy spent the next two days in bed. Bernadette came to him after midnight, and his infection cleared up as he got used to her. He went back to patrolling the streets when he could piss like a man.

ONE DAY OUT of nowhere, Billy's brother Frank appeared. Frank's circumstances had changed since he'd worked at the Burlington shops in Havelock. He'd inherited some money and quit his job. Their mother was now bedridden, and Frank had the legal guardianship. He'd sold land and bought stock in a company called International Business Machines. He'd picked it because he liked the word "International."

Frank showed up driving a shiny new De Soto. The car had a V8 engine, and Frank took Billy out and pushed it to 100. He stepped on the gas to prove it would go faster, then let it coast back down to the speed limit. "Fee's faft," Frank said, "but what I'd really like to fee iv thif big fuckin' engine in a Ftudebaker."

"You'd have to change the suspension," Billy groused. "You wouldn't be able to keep it on the road." The Ford he used as a patrol car would do 95 at best.

Frank had decided, after studying a book of photographs, that Indians were America's proletariat. Billy introduced him to Gerard, and the two of them loaded the De Soto's trunk with beer and headed for South Dakota, with Bernadette riding along in the back seat. Billy watched with mixed feelings as she waved goodbye from the rear window. He was glad his brother was gone, but seeing Bernadette with them made him anxious. He hoped they wouldn't wreck the car with her in it.

He remembered that Ruth had invited him and called her. She said he could come on Sunday. The meal would be late, but he was welcome and she'd put on an extra potato. On Saturday, he bought a bottle of Mogen David wine. Billy drank little himself—he liked a beer occasionally—but he knew it was proper to bring something. He did not care for sour-tasting Portuguese vin rosé.

"Goodneff," she said when she heard Frank had been in town. "You mufft have been furprived and ecffited."

"Frank's my brother." Billy shrugged. "He's the same as always, only richer."

"Some of that money should have been yours, you know," she said.

Billy and Ruth's husband tolerated one another. Conversation at the table was not scintillating. Ruth poured more wine, mostly for herself, and asked Billy what he did all week. He told them about his latest incident, the shooting of a rabid skunk, and how he'd carried the corpse at the end of a bamboo fishing pole, so that drips of its skunk oil ran down the pole and got onto his fingers.

George Smith looked amused. "Did you use your police revolver? There couldn't have been much skunk left."

"The revolver was all I had with me."

"What did you do with the carcass?"

"I had them burn it in the hospital incinerator."

"Do you ever put up targets for target practice?" the couple's son asked. Ruth's kid was a foot taller than a normal ten-year-old, with a lip-suture similar to Billy's.

"Sometimes I go out to the dump to shoot at rats," Billy said. "I've yet to hit one."

"I wish I had a BB gun," the kid said. "I'd shoot that dumb orange cat that lives next door."

"Maybe that's why you don't have one," George Smith said.

After supper they played rummy. The boy won, then went off to his bedroom to read the encyclopedia. George Smith excused himself, left the table, pushed back in his recliner, and began snoring in less than five minutes. "You see how it goes," Ruth moaned, clutching at her temples. "I am in despair."

"You've done a great job decorating," Billy said, glancing around the combined living-and-dining-rooms for evidence.

She let go of her hair and hid her lovely face in her hands. "Ruth Smith," she said. "What kind of a name is that?" He reached out to take her wrist, but she drew back with a hiss. "Don't you *dare* touch me! I never should have invited you."

Frank and Gerard came back from South Dakota on Monday. The De Soto that bounded over the curb and into Billy's front yard had aged five years. The undercarriage was snagged with grass, and the fenders were scraped and smeared as if the car had been crashed through plum thickets. The passenger-side door sprang open and Gerard fell out. He staggered to his feet and began dragging Billy's brother from the back seat. On the driver's side of the car, Bernadette sat behind the steering wheel, blinking and scowling. "I got 'em," Gerard said, though Billy had not offered to help. Gerard lifted Frank in a shoulder carry, lurched backward, and sat down in the dust.

"Better let me do it." Billy hunkered down and draped Frank's arm across his shoulder, then lifted him and walked him into the house. He laid him on the couch and went back out to see whether Bernadette was as drunk as the others. She was out of the car, trying to drag Gerard to his feet. "Help me lift," she said, stumbling under the big man's weight. "He's too heavy."

"What happened?" Billy asked her. "How did the car get so messed up?" He took Gerard's arm, and they guided him toward the trailer, though Bernadette was no less wobbly than the two men. "You stink," he said to her. There was vomit in her blueblack hair and her breath was sweet like radiator antifreeze.

"Fuck the car." Her eyes were dark and wild. "Whose place is that? I don't want to go in there."

"It's your trailer. Yours and Gerard's."

"No it isn't," she said. "It must be yours."

Frank left the next morning without a word about proletarian Indians. In the weeks that followed, Billy saw himself trapped between two women, one six years older and one barely more than a child. Ruth met him in the daytime, twice in the following month. Bernadette wrapped him in her spaghetti limbs at night. "Help me," each seemed to be saying. "Do something." But Billy didn't know how to do anything, other than operate a machine gun.

BILLY ASSUMED GERARD knew Bernadette was sleeping with him. He found out he was mistaken one hot August night when a heavy pounding brought him to the door. "Where's my sister?" Gerard demanded in a high, choked voice. "Where is she?"

"She's here," Billy said in a reasoned tone. "Give us one minute."

"Like hell," Gerard said. "Where is she?" He gripped Billy's undershirt and lifted him until it tore; he pivoted, threw Billy into the yard, and charged on into the house.

"God damn it." Billy picked himself up and went in after Gerard. A splintering came from within as a door lost its hinges. Gerard's back loomed ahead of him in the dark; Billy leaped like a cat to put the sleeper hold on him, but Gerard shook him off the way a dog shakes off water. Bernadette screamed, and Billy remembered his bayonet in the kitchen drawer. Before he could act, Gerard dragged the girl past him, smashing him aside and against the wall. Billy leaped onto Gerard's back again. As he was being carried out into the yard, Billy extended his thumb and struck Gerard's throat from the

63

side; his thumbnail failed to penetrate, and he felt the joint pop. Meanwhile Bernadette clutched a pillow in her free hand and beat her brother with it. Gerard grabbed it from her and ripped it open, and feathers floated on the midnight air. "I told you!" he shouted. "I told you to stay away from him." He slapped her so hard that Billy thought her neck would be broken.

"You can't do that," Billy said from the big man's back. "You're under arrest."

Gerard turned his head and gave Billy his attention. "Fuck you. You ought to be ashamed." Billy dropped to his feet and tried a kick at the man's kidney; Gerard punched him straight in the forehead, and the front yard filled with a thousand blinking fireflies. In the minute or so that followed, Billy clawed at Gerard's bulk, but his hatred felt absurd, as if he were trying to punish a sofa. Later came the sensation of floating and slamming into things; sometimes he collided with the house, sometimes the ground. He felt more of a jolting than physical pain, and he felt furious with his body because it wasn't fighting back. He remembered seeing Bernadette, nude, clinging to her brother's leg, and, later, Gerard looking thoughtfully down at him. It was Rudy McDonough who drove him to the hospital.

"You look like shit," the doctor said to him. "How's that bladder infection?"

All the pain caught up with him the next day. It had taken eight stitches to close the cut above his eye; his nose was broken, along with his thumb and a couple of ribs. His shoulder was dislocated but not separated. Nobody at the hospital had asked what happened; they only poked him and bent his joints to see which ones hurt. Because he couldn't drive, he missed two weeks of work; the city clerk paid him anyway, but took two weeks out of his vacation.

The upshot was that he lost Ruth for a time, though Bernadette came to him in the early hours, just as before the fight. Billy ordered a six-cell flashlight from the back of a barbershop magazine. This flashlight, manufactured in Alabama, had a nine-volt bulb and a beam like a locomotive, but the most wonderful thing was the sliding mass of its batteries. Because they were loosely stacked, not jammed tight inside the tube (aluminum, heavy duty, guaranteed not to dent or bend), their weight was advertised to have a dead-blow effect, similar to the birdshot inside a blackjack.

While he waited for his flashlight to arrive, Billy made amends with Gerard, who now treated him as a brother-in-law and invited him to go fishing. The next time he had to arrest the giant Indian, Gerard came along cheerfully, and Billy lent him a blanket for his cell bunk and gave him money to pay his fine. By the time school started in September, Ruth and Billy were meeting one another again. It was as if they were cursed. Then one day George Smith hired Bernadette to watch his and Ruth's son after school.

That was too much for Ruth. She fumed like gasoline in a pail, ready for the match.

"I don't know what you see in the little twat," Ruth said one day. "She's nothing but a, a darkness. She won't lift her hand to wash a single dish. She steals my pills."

"Let's not talk about her," Billy said. "Since it upsets you."

"You're the one who upsets me," she said. "Just wait till she gets fat and pregnant."

"She won't do that. Bernadette is different."

"She's a woman. I'm a woman. You're a fool."

At the time of Ruth's comment, Bernadette had missed two periods. She told him, finally, and they rose early one morning and Billy drove her to the Indian Health Service up in South Dakota. The doctor there glanced at her, shrugged, and took her to an examination room while Billy sat in the waiting area and watched little round-faced kids attack the magazines. "We'll run a test," the doctor said when he came out. "I can tell you what the results will be."

"Can you do anything?" Billy had worn his constable's uniform so the visit would look official. Even so, the doctor backed away as from a snake. "I mean—"

"I know what you mean," the doctor said. "The answer is no."

Bernadette came out looking flustered and skeletal. On the way to the exit she tried to take his hand. "Don't do that. It doesn't look good," he said. "People think I'm on duty."

"That doctor was ugly to me," she said, "and so are you."

Billy strode to the car in silence. He didn't want the girl alongside him where he would see her profile. "How come you never want to get drunk?" Bernadette asked as she trotted to catch up. "What's the matter with you?"

"I can't talk right now."

Billy was seeing his future narrowed to Turtle Lodge. He had planned on moving to Hollywood, maybe becoming an actor in one of the cop shows there. He wanted to take Ruth with him, but when he'd mentioned it, she'd laughed. "You an actor? You couldn't entertain a goldfish. Besides, if you hadn't noticed, I have a son to raise."

He also saw this: once Bernadette began to show, Ruth would have nothing more to do with him.

Bernadette did not look pregnant until after Thanksgiving; even then, a person would have had to be watching for it. She needed a winter coat, and of course she had no money. George Smith came to the rescue. He had ordered Ruth an expensive red wool coat from Sears and Roebuck, but she called him a tasteless fool and refused to wear it. So, he brought the coat to Billy, knowing he would pass it on to Bernadette. Bernadette loved the coat and wore it indoors and out, though it made her look like a young girl playing dress-up. The sight of Bernadette wearing Ruth's coat made Billy's head spin.

Evidently it had a similar effect on Ruth, because she pitched a tantrum and demanded that the coat be retrieved. Billy dug into his savings and bought a nice-looking black coat for Bernadette, and one morning he slipped out with the red coat in hand and turned it over to George. When he got back to his house, he found the girl with his bayonet in her grip. She had slashed the new coat to ribbons, and now she turned on him. "I'll get you a red one, I'll get you a red one," he said as he backed away, out of breath and holding both her wrists. Her black hair tangled in her face.

"It's not the coat," she said as she tore herself free from him. "You stupid idiot cop boy, you don't know anything."

"But you need a coat," he pleaded. "You're going to be cold."

"Cold? I'll melt the snow in front of me. Your idiot cop boy baby makes me hot as a furnace."

He bought her another red coat that cost him two weeks' pay, the reddest he could find in the stores on Main Street. Sometimes she wore it, more often she did not. Then December arrived, and the weather turned deadly.

THE PATROL CAR had a six-volt electrical system. If the engine got chilled it wouldn't start, so Billy had to drive the black-and-white home at the end of his shift. He would set his alarm for five a.m. and go out in the cold and warm it up. Interrupted sleep made him revisit the retreat down the Korean peninsula, when they'd been sniped at from the ridges in the daytime and mortared at night. Some nights he woke with a gasp, fighting the girl who clung to him. He carried jumper cables in case a citizen needed a boost, but for the newer cars with their twelve-volt systems there was nothing he could do. He suggested that the city purchase a new patrol car, but the city clerk laughed.

Unheard-of events took place because of the cold. A cross-country Freightways truck stopped dead on the highway, its diesel fuel turned to jelly. A cow froze upright in the corner of a pasture. A farmhouse on the edge of town exploded and burned; the column of smoke could be seen from the next town east. One citizen who needed her car started was Althea Dodson. "Come inside and warm yourself up," she suggested. "I've made chocolate chip cookies." After they had fucked in her preferred manner—hard and steady until she moaned—he collapsed on her soft breasts, weeping, while she rubbed his crew-cut head. "There, there. That's a good boy."

"Something's the matter with me," he sobbed. "I think I'm losing my mind."

"This whole town is losing its mind. It's because of the wind."

He had double dreams in which waking was part of the dream. He would be sitting in a foxhole with his feet in ice, watching his precious comic books slip down into the mud, and he would think, "I know this dream. I've had it before." He would force himself awake, to find himself in his upstairs room in Lincoln, with his brother coming in past midnight, stinking of puke and politics and dropping his boots on the floor. Then his alarm would go off—time to start the car—and it would wake him from a dream of waiting for the alarm.

The county sheriff's office handled all dispatch calls so that the city wouldn't have to pay a dispatcher or buy a radio. One late afternoon when the weather was at its coldest, Billy came on shift in time for a call. He was to go and break up a fight. The address was familiar. He drove to Ruth's and parked the patrol car in the driveway. Shrill female voices came from inside the house. Somebody inside was beating on a door, boom boom boom boom boom. A cat-o'-nine-tails wind blew a wisp of dry snow across the windshield.

He left the motor running and got out and went around to the entry at the front of the house. With his heart ringing like an anvil, he opened the screen, went up the one low step, and pushed open the inside door. There was his cousin, wild as a captured deer, bashing the kitchen door with the heel of a boot. "Let me through, let me through!" she screamed. "Let me through so I can strangle you with your own greasy hair!"

"Ruth! Stop!" Billy said, going up to her. "Stop and take a breath. There's no need."

"It's about time you came," she said, panting. "I order you to arrest a thief. She has taken my valuable coat. She is wearing the evidence."

"Who has taken it?" Billy asked, though he knew the answer.

"Who the God-damn fuck do you think? Your damned pathetic little prostitute, that's who took it, and I'll get it back if I have to cut it off her."

"Control yourself. Bernadette is not a prostitute."

"Don't defend her to *me*, you leg-humping puppy!" Ruth threatened him with the boot. "Shoot her! What do you have a gun for? She's a thief! I caught her in the act! Shoot her!"

Billy felt himself go pale. Something was wrong with Ruth's green eyes. Her pupils were dark windows into an empty room.

"You want me to shoot her over a coat?"

"She's taken all sorts of things. She steals my medicine." Ruth tried to grab his revolver from its holster. "Give me the fucking gun. I'll shoot her myself."

"Don't *do* that." Billy shoved her hand away. "Stop acting crazy and take a good deep breath. I'm not here to shoot anybody."

"I am not crazy! Don't you dare ever call me crazy!"

"All right," he said. "All right, now. Let's calm down." He turned aside from her to examine the door. It was a two-way pass-through, with a brass plate in place of a knob. It fit the opening too tightly for him to hook it with a finger. "Does the side door lock?"

"It has a ten-cent barrel latch. A child could kick it open."

"We'll go around that way, then." As they passed back through the house, Billy was aware of being observed. Ruth's tall prepubescent son stood in the doorway of a spare room next to the entry. His eyes were brown, alert, the pupils narrow, taking in everything.

Billy and Ruth skirted the front of the patrol car and ran to the rear of the house; the boy followed. The kitchen door was locked. Billy turned the knob and shoved the door with his shoulder, and it broke free and opened inward. They found the kitchen vacated. The door to the living room had swung the other way—a coat rack lay propping it open—and Billy looked through in time to see Bernadette exit the front entry, wearing the blood-red coat. He hurdled the fallen coat rack and sprinted after her, hoping to catch her before she reached the patrol car, but the screen door got in his way—it opened toward him—and she was already in the passenger's seat when he came out. She shot him a dark look and slapped the door locks down. "Bernadette, honey, the coat's not yours. You have to give it up." The girl ignored him.

"Shoot out a window," Ruth said, coming up behind him. "Drag her by the hair."

"Keep quiet and keep away from me. I need you to please step back inside the house."

"Don't boss me," she said. "This driveway is my property."

"Damn you both." He chewed the edge of his thumb. "You could have settled this yourselves. Have pity on me, Ruth." But he saw no mercy in her ice-green eyes.

Ruth sighed. "I'll go back in," she said at last. "But you better get me my coat."

"I wish I'd never seen that coat. The label must say 'Made in Hell.'"

"Don't blame the coat. Everything that's happened is because of you."

To Billy, what took place during the next five hours would be a puzzle whose pieces did not fit. It was like the flow of battle, where ten thousand things happened at once that might be recalled later in detail but that could never be placed in a rational order. That day, that night, he could only act; later, whether he tried to remember or to forget, he would be haunted by a staccato slideshow of horrific Kodachromes.

He drove Bernadette to his house and wrestled the red coat off her, but the second he turned his back she put it on again and ran out into the yard. He chased her down and carried her inside, while she kicked and scratched and slashed at him with her hard little fists. Indoors it turned into a real fight, with no quarter being given on either side, and before long each of them was winded. Billy had an athlete's build, and he was tall and fit and twice her size and weight, but Bernadette fought in a trance, with the strength of demons. He bruised her wrists; she brought blood to his lip. A whirlwind of hate blew into the house and spun them both into the kitchen.

The bayonet came to her hand first. Now it, rather than the coat, became the focus of their struggle. Bernadette gripped the handle with

Billy's hands over hers, and they swung each other like a couple at a barnyard dance. He tried lifting it above his head to put it beyond her reach, and she twisted within his arms and pressed her back to him. She gave a scream, the blade came down and in, and suddenly the house was quiet.

The abrupt silence was palpable. Bernadette fell back against him and relaxed, her dark head weighing on his neck, his tender arms around her, holding her upright.

He quickly propped her against the refrigerator. Shaking like an epileptic, his hands weak as a baby's, Billy knelt before her and fumbled at her coat. With her last strength she clutched the lapels and hugged the red coat to her. Bernadette's eyes were open and staring down at him, first in defiance and then with surprise and wonder. "Oh, God, honey," he said, and she said, "Don't—" Then the light went out of her gaze and she slid toward the floor.

The girl never looked more beautiful than when he carried her to the car. Her hair fell across his wrist, light and cool to the touch, and flowed against his skin as smooth as river water. Her plum-ripe lips, full and sweet but paler than before, were parted, and long black lashes veiled her half-closed eyes. The bayonet's haft poking up beneath her coat felt wrong, like some awful prosthesis. He laid her in the back seat of the patrol car and drove straight to the hospital. When he got there, he found she had slid down into the well behind the front seat. She had somehow gotten folded in a way that hid her from view. He lifted her hand to rouse her, but her touch felt as dry as a lizard's.

Billy knew death when it met his skin, having watched it creep toward his foxhole in the winter moonlight, having heard it come to men around him, having inhaled its stinking cabbage-eater's breath and very nearly tasted it, too. Nevertheless he checked her pulse. There was no blood pressure. He dropped her cold hand with a shudder.

He understood that it looked as if he'd killed her. (Had he killed her, or had she killed herself? They had done it together.) He knew he could go to prison, even if she was only an Indian, even if he could persuade the jury that it was manslaughter done in self-defense. He tucked the red coat over her body and closed the door, and got in the driver's seat and left the ambulance apron, and began to drive. He drove the patrol car around every snowy block, up and down every ice-slick street. He avoided stop signs and kept moving, waving with two gloved fingers to the people on their way to supper at the Pendergast or the Milestone, not stopping to talk to anybody, at times half sick to his stomach, at other times trying to hide a crazy laugh. He suddenly saw that, for as long he could get gasoline, he could drive and drive and drive and never stop. Free of Ruth and free of Bernadette, free at last of Turtle Lodge and its city clerk and its Althea Dodsons and Wendy Kugelmans, he could drive the length of the hemisphere and start over in South America.

He recognized an insane thought—maybe Ruth would meet him in Rio de Janeiro—and he understood he'd stepped through a mirror, and that his new life as a criminal had begun.

BILLY HAD READ his share of detective novels, and he knew how a murderer was supposed to think. First, he should conceal the murder weapon; Baldwin McDonough, among others, could trace the bayonet to him. Next, he should get rid of the body. He should try to frame somebody— why not Ruth's husband? He could kill two birds with one stone, so to speak—for the murder. But driving around town with a corpse hidden under a coat rendered him all but incapable of scheming. He caught himself gazing at nothing, guiding the car like a sleepwalker.

George Smith. George Smith. Billy knew the Smith family routine. Ruth was at home; he'd just seen her there; she had gotten off from her courthouse job at five o'clock. The kid would still be in because of the cold. George Smith handled grain in the fall, but most of his business was hauling cattle over into Iowa, a trip that took from ten to twelve hours. He could be expected back in Turtle Lodge at any time after six-thirty. Smith would dolly down his trailer out at the truck barn south of town and bobtail to their house to eat his supper. Then he'd drive back out to park his tractor indoors, where its engine would stay warm enough to start again in the morning. Billy had to stay unavailable until Smith got his precious diesel put away and drove his straight-eight Buick back to town. Once Billy saw the Buick pulled up behind Ruth's Chevy, he could place Bernadette's body at the truck barn, "hidden" where it could easily be found.

Smith employed a part-time mechanic, a sandhills-born Negro who worked days at the Ford garage. Watson, the mechanic, always checked the truck barn's heater before midnight, and it would be convenient if he found the body then. That left Billy a window of as much as three hours to lose the murder weapon and what was left of Bernadette.

Six-thirty, then seven, then eight o'clock passed with no sign of Smith's semi, either at the truck barn or in the parking lot of the Milestone; a pair of cross-country truckers waited out the night, plumes of vapor drifting up from their idling rigs, but Smith did not pull in. The minutes dragged, and Billy started to feel panicky. It was his long-standing prayer that George Smith would drive into a bridge, but he knew that, on a night like this, it was more likely that something had gone wrong with the truck. There was no indication of alarm at Ruth's house.

The streets were empty except for Second Street in front of the Pleasant Hour, where the women's bowling league was still competing. Business at the bars and at the Elks Club was down. No teenagers cruised the streets. Billy was alone except for the presence behind the seat. He reached back a few times to shake Bernadette's cold wrist. Her limbs were taking on *rigor mortis* per deadman's schedule.

Desperate finally, he drove south out of town past the truck barn, where Smith's frost-blind Buick waited for its owner. The turnoff to Smith and Son came just after the City Limit sign, on the Baxter's Pond side of the unpaved highway. Distance to the nearest houses was half a block, and none faced the property directly. Billy thought of a hiding place for the bayonet—he could tuck it up under the seat of a used-out truck cab that sat among weeds near a pile of scrap welding-iron—but he had second thoughts about planting Bernadette's body. Suppose he left it and Smith got home late after all, and found Bernadette and called it in? Nobody would then suspect Smith.

Nobody would suspect him anyway. George Smith didn't have the imagination or the time to murder a teenaged girl and hide her body. If the townspeople suspected anyone, it would be the Negro mechanic. Billy cursed all authors of detective fiction. Their kind of stupid-ass plan might work in London or San Francisco, but it wouldn't work in Turtle Lodge, where everybody knew everybody and knew what they were capable of. For that matter, it never seemed to work in novels, either.

Still, he had to get rid of her somehow. Billy had already gone the first five miles toward Rio; now he turned the patrol car back toward town and swung it into the truck barn's driveway. He opened the rear-seat door and lifted the flap of the coat. Bernadette was doubled tight around her midriff, and she had already stiffened considerably, so that it was difficult to reach the bayonet's haft. Billy got a grip on it—the thing was slippery—but it didn't want to budge. He jerked and pulled, but it was as if he were trying to remove one of her bones. Finally he tore it free; he ran to the junked-out cab at the side of the truck barn and opened the driver's-side door. There was plenty of space under the seat, but he wasn't satisfied. He reached beneath the seat to feel the springs, and found a place to slip the flat of the blade up under the wires. A voice in his ear whispered *Fingerprints, fool! Fingerprints!* He had nothing to wipe it down with but blood or urine. He would have to come back later, when the coast was clear.

He thought to leave Bernadette in the truck cab, too; he could prop her behind the steering wheel as a kind of joke. But as he ran back to the patrol car, a pickup truck rattled by on its slow way south toward one of the ranches. Billy's breath stopped and his knees began to shake—he hadn't had much composure anyway—and he got back into the patrol car and gripped the wheel with trembling hands. He had to rid himself of the corpse somehow, but if the pickup's driver had seen him at the truck barn, to leave it there just then would be a huge mistake.

Billy drove a mile, following the pickup south. It crossed his mind to simply keep driving, but the cop car was low on gas, and it was the most conspicuous getaway vehicle he could imagine. He turned the car around and drove back north, passing the truck barn again, and continued straight ahead up Main Street. There was still nothing happening in the town, except for the women's bowling league at the Pleasant Hour. If this had been a normal night, Billy might hide behind the Pleasant Hour to wait for drunks.

Indians used the alley behind the Pleasant Hour Lanes and Tables to get from the downtown bars (they couldn't legally go inside, but they could wait in the freezing shadows for shadowy transactions) to their shacks on the south side of town. Acting on impulse, Billy turned the patrol car up the alley, stopped and got out, and quickly tumbled Bernadette's stiff body from the car. She was as awkward to shift as the carcass of a frozen deer, and he had to partially uncurl her. Where he had jerked the weapon out of her, there was not much additional fresh blood, but she had left a sticky lake in the well behind the front seat.

He lifted and dragged her fifty feet up the alley, to the concrete apron behind the Pleasant Hour. Soon the small lump that had been his lover lay beneath her coat like a pillowcase of laundry. For a moment, shame and pity flooded him, and he stepped back to the patrol car and stood there paralyzed. He had arrived at a place of desolation and could go no further. The bitter wind licked at his collar.

Then he heard the scrape of uneven footsteps.

Billy retrieved his flashlight from the patrol car and flicked the switch. The bloom of light showed Gerard Horse Looking, stumbling toward him and holding up an enormous crooked-fingered hand to protect his eyes. Gerard lurched to a stop and Billy went to meet him, making sure to keep the beam trained on his face.

"Hey, Billy, 's that you, man? Hey, gi' me a ride to m' trailer. It's fuckin' cold."

"I'll give you a ride," Billy said. "Let me help you to the car." He snapped off the switch, flipped the flashlight and caught it, and stroked Gerard across his temple. The big man dropped like a sack of potatoes.

Billy dragged Gerard off to the side so his patrol car could pass. Gerard was a godsend. Gerard could shoulder the blame for his sister's death. All Billy had to do was to rush back out to the truck barn and retrieve the bayonet. Once he had "found" the two Horse Lookings and the bayonet, he could bloody Gerard and arrest him, or he could pull Bernadette's body back into the car. That way, the blood in the patrol car would be accounted for. He would leave the bayonet at the scene and tell everyone Gerard must have stolen it from him. Billy's forehead pounded and his heart jumped with glee.

That's when Wendy Kugelman telephoned the dispatcher to say that her pilot light was out.

"*I don't have time for this shit!*" Billy screamed into the microphone. "Who does that woman think I am, the fucking gas company? Mobile unit over."

"There's no gas company in Turtle Lodge. It'll be a propane furnace," came the calm reply. "Base over."

"All right," Billy said. "You can tell the dried-up bitch I'm on my way. Mobile unit over."

"Shame on you, Billy Dixon. Wendy says you're always so polite. Base unit clear."

The microphone stuck to his glove. He looked down, saw that his sleeve was covered in blood, and realized that all along he'd been leaving blood on the steering wheel and shift lever. The cuff of his jacket was soaked, as was the crotch of his uniform pants. Billy raced the five blocks to his house, left the patrol car with the engine running, and cleaned himself as best he could, changing his uniform pants for jeans and his bloody cop boots for running shoes. The leather jacket cleaned up all right except for the knitted cuff, which he soaped and rinsed in the bathroom sink. When he glanced down, he saw that the floor beneath his feet was pink. He put down newspaper, cleaned the soles of his tennis shoes with more newspaper, and ran back to the car. Before getting in, he used a hot wet dishrag to wipe the controls and vinyl seat covers.

Wendy Kugelman owned a small house north of the highway. Over there on the north side, where the rich had built their ranch-style homes, there was a block that ought to have been relocated south of the tracks. A scrapyard took up a half-block in the middle, with a board fence around three sides. The row of tiny houses whose back windows looked out on the fence was called Ileyville, for John Iley, the owner of the scrapyard. Billy parked the patrol car in the middle of the block and approached a pink house whose bare rosebushes juddered in the wind. *Damn her*, he thought, *why couldn't she have called a plumber?* If Wendy's furnace was out, it was out, but her timing was terrible.

The front door opened before he could knock. Wendy stood there in her fuzzy pink housecoat, huddled up and shivering. Her cold house felt hot to Billy after the slashing wind outdoors; he chafed his bare wrist where the frozen cuff had burned it. "I'm here," he said gruffly, avoiding her anxious eyes. "Is it in the basement?"

"It's a floor furnace in the bedroom," she said with a note of resentment. "What's the matter? Don't you want to help me?"

"It's been a crazy night," he said. "Show me where it is. I need to keep moving."

Wendy gave a refined little European shrug. "If you'll forgive my untidiness." She led the way to her room, where photographs and female accoutrements crowded every surface.

The furnace was let into the floor near the turned-down bed. Billy knelt and placed his ear close to the grille. "I don't hear a flame," he said. "Where are your matches?" He lifted the cold steel grate that gave access to the controls. "Did you check your propane tank?"

"Here," Wendy said, handing him the matchbox. "I had it filled last week. I would have tried to light it, but I was afraid."

Billy removed the wingnut that secured the sight glass, twisted an unlit kitchen match into the match holder, struck a second match to light the first, held the button, and reached down into the cavity with the holder to light the pilot. He counted to thirty and released the button, and the small flame danced and purred. "The wind's gone down a bit," he said, replacing the cap that held the sight glass. "You should be OK now." He turned the control knob to the *on* position, and the burner lit with a *whoof*. "There. Done." He fastened the sight glass, replaced the steel grate, and stood up.

"Don't go yet," Wendy Kugelman said. "I have to thank you." Of course she was opening her robe. Billy turned to look in spite of himself, in time to watch a horrible transformation. Wendy's soft blondish hair became long and straight and black; her face got younger and browner, with high-sculpted cheekbones and burning upslanted eyes; her pale lips moistened and turned chokecherry-colored, and her pink housecoat became red. Bernadette Horse Looking stood before him. The coat she held open revealed her abdomen, slit from navel to pubis and spread apart; her rubbery intestines bulged, and blood ran down her thighs.

"NO!" Billy shrieked. "I DIDN'T MEAN IT! KEEP AWAY FROM ME!" He bolted past the pink dresser with its frou-frou and fragrances, out the front door and into the wind, where no suffocating pinkness surrounded him. Canadian air poured south, and the white stars looked down on a world locked in ice. To the east, a little north of the highway, the shoulder of Turtle Lodge Butte bulked upward, darker than the night.

"I didn't mean it, I didn't mean it," he repeated, but no one was listening.

THE RADIO POPPED with static as he got into the car. "—*driveway back of the Pleasant Hour*," the dispatcher was saying. "*Step on it*."

"Ten-four." Billy hurried to be the first cop there. More would come, Starchy Sedgwick for sure and probably the two stateys. He needed to get to Gerard before the others. He had plans for him.

He turned on the flashing roof light but not the siren and crossed the highway without stopping. There were no taillights ahead of him in the alley. Two pin-boys and the city clerk stood by Bernadette's body. Billy's headlights picked out Gerard lying where he'd left him, and he passed up

Bernadette and the city clerk and stopped the patrol car with a screech of brakes.

"Over here," the clerk called out. "This girl's been stabbed."

"And here's the S. O. B. who did it." Billy jumped out with his flashlight and ran and grabbed Gerard by the collar. The big man's neck felt warm, though there was no response when Billy shined the light in his eyes. "Wake up, you drunk bastard," he said loud enough for the clerk to hear, and began dragging Gerard toward the patrol car.

"What are you doing?" the city clerk shouted. "This girl needs taken to the hospital!"

"Then call the ambulance," Billy shouted back. "Can't you see I'm trying to make an arrest?" In a frenzy of effort, he skidded Gerard toward the rear of the patrol car, yanked open the back door, propped the big man up, smacked him across the nose with his flashlight, and shoved his head in over the sill. *Bleed for me, my friend*, he thought. *For God's sake, bleed.*

The city clerk came running and grabbed him by the arm. "Stop what you're doing, you stupid shit," he said. "We're trying to save a girl's life here."

"The dispatcher told me she was dead."

"I never said that," the clerk said. "We don't know that. Come and take a look."

Billy let go of Gerard's collar, and the comatose giant rolled out of the car and lay face up. His broken nose bled a little, though Billy had hoped for more. Billy turned and followed the city clerk to Bernadette's corpse, where he went through the motions of searching for life. "She's stiff," he reported. "Probably been here a while. She's dead, all right."

"We'll take her to the hospital anyway," the city clerk said. "Take that big fellow, too."

"Take him? You're crazy," Billy said. "I'm taking his ass to jail. He can sober up there."

"You're taking him to the hospital," the clerk said. "What if he has hypothermia and dies in custody? You'll land us in the middle of a federal investigation. You better remember who signs your paychecks."

The ambulance crew showed up for Bernadette. While they and the clerk were fussing over her corpse, Billy returned to the patrol car. He lifted Gerard and shoved his torso into the back seat, then handcuffed his arms behind him and crouched to heave the rest of him in. Gerard was heavy as a cow; no reflexes, no response. At one point he let out a sigh, so

Billy knew he was breathing. *Maybe I should smother him,* he thought. *Who knows if he saw anything?*

Just then the city clerk came over; the ambulance was leaving with Bernadette. "You take that man straight to the emergency entrance," he said. "No more monkey business with the flashlight. Jesus Christ, you got blood on his shirt. Look at that!" Rather than a heavy coat or insulated jacket, Gerard wore a heavy flannel shirt against the cold.

Billy said, "That blood is hers."

"Maybe it is hers, dimwit," the clerk said. "Can you swear it's not his in front of a jury? No, you can't."

Back in the warmth of the patrol car once more, Billy considered what the clerk had said. Rather than the risk of a trial by jury, where any dumb thing could go awry, it would be better for him if Gerard were dead. He should smother the big Indian now. Then he remembered the hallucination in Wendy's bedroom and shivered. He had a weak mind, evidently. If he killed the girl's brother, seeing the two of them together would really make him crazy.

He delivered Gerard Horse Looking to the hospital. After midnight, the dispatcher called him back to the alley, where he pretended to search for the murder weapon. Starchy Sedgwick and the two state highway patrolmen were on the case by then, and the city clerk kept them all there till daylight. Billy longed to blurt, "Give me ten minutes and I'll get it for you," but he clamped his mouth shut and endured the farce. His toes in the canvas shoes hurt terribly. His wet wrist got frostbitten and itched and peeled for a month.

George Smith spent that cold night in Iowa, Billy found out later, in a soft bed in an overheated motel room. Coming home in his empty cattle truck, he'd run over a two-by-four lying in the roadway. He had ruined three brand-new tires, but he hadn't hit a bridge. He hadn't even skidded off the pavement.

Tildy

IT WAS FEBRUARY, no sign yet of anything but winter, the wind from South Dakota still colder than a dead girl's kiss. Billy Dixon sat in the parking lot of the Milestone, sipping his first free coffee of the evening. He was thinking about the upcoming trial of Gerard Horse Looking when the dispatcher got him on the radio. ". . . Miriam Stamforth residence to investigate a report of a baby crying, base over."

Billy set his coffee cup on the floormat and picked up the ice-cold microphone. "Say again, please? Mobile unit over."

"The old crank thinks she hears a baby crying in her garage. You need to check it out. She's a big contributor to the library fund. Do you copy? Over."

"Ten-four, I copy Stamforth residence, one baby in one garage. Mobile unit clear." The '50 Ford patrol car's blower barely kept the windshield open, and the coffee steam wasn't helping. Billy poured what was left in the cup back into his Thermos bottle and peered through the fogged glass. The highway was empty, no cattle trucks, no cars, so he pulled out onto it and headed west toward the oldest side of town. One good thing about this call, Mrs. Stamforth was not likely to seduce him.

The Stamforth house was decayed and tall, the kind of gables-and-gingerbread palace that the rich once built; high windows gave onto double-decker porches. The face that scowled up at him past the edge of the heavy door seemed to be made of compressed powdered donuts. She held it open far enough to extend a sugary claw. "Back there," she said in the voice of an owl, and gestured toward the side of the house. "Whatever is making that sound, you need to put a stop to it."

Carrying his six-cell flashlight, Billy followed the brick driveway to a garage that had been built when Buicks were tall and narrow. He paused at the front of it to listen; he heard nothing at first, but then a painful hiccupping wail came from within. He went around to the side, where a narrow walkway led to a door, and turned the loose porcelain knob. Rather than a car from the 1920s, he found the narrow space all but filled by an ancient fire truck.

"Wra-a-a-aagh!" The voice sounded human, but no baby could survive the temperatures of the past few weeks. Billy switched on his flashlight and probed underneath the seats. When he shined it under the dash of the truck, a green pair of eyes blazed back at him. They belonged to a scrawny and brindled kitten, no more than two-thirds grown. It was panting and appeared to be in distress.

"Here, kitty." Billy stretched forth a gloved hand, with his fingers cupped as if holding a treat. The kitten leaned closer to sniff, and he quickly slapped his hand over it, pinning its neck. The kitten fought crazily, but Billy was well gauntleted, and when he lifted it by the scruff, the animal went rigid. He dragged it into the light for a better look. Four white feet, clean needle-sharp teeth. It stretched its claws toward him and spat.

"Aren't you the mighty featherweight. Here, don't bite me." Billy eased back out of the garage, careful not to relax his grip. He switched off the beam and tucked his flashlight under his belt, and carried the kitten up the driveway toward his patrol car. As he passed the parlor window, Mrs. Stamforth peeked out. Billy held the cat up for her to see. She snatched the curtain shut.

"Mmwra-a-a-auggh."

"You don't have to yell at me. Not everything around here is my fault."

Billy had come on shift at four, and he figured the veterinarian's office out on the highway would still be open. By the time he arrived, the kitten had quit fighting, and he was able to carry it tucked inside his uniform jacket. The girl at the desk looked up at the bulge. "What do we have here? A stray?"

"I assume so," Billy said, unzipping. "I took it out of Mrs. Stamforth's garage."

"Do you want us to put it down? If we do, the city will have to reimburse us. Old Lady Stamforth never pays for anything."

"I don't know. Let me think for a second." Billy set the cat on the counter, where it gave another bloodcurdling yell. "Something's wrong with it."

"I bet I know what's wrong." The girl began stroking the back of the starved animal, and it crouched with its rear held high and vibrated its tail. "We're a little female, aren't we?" the girl said. "And we're having a little female complaint."

"You think she's in heat? She doesn't seem old enough."

"House cats start reproducing as early as eighteen weeks. What do you want us to do here? We are closing."

Billy removed a glove and reached to touch the kitten's head. "She's pretty," he said, though it would have been more correct to say she had potential. "Do you have to put her down?"

"We don't have to do anything," the girl said. "But if you turn her outside in this weather, she's going to die."

"How much does it cost to spay a cat?"

"For you, ten dollars. That includes her shots. We'll feed her and keep her warm until she settles down. We don't like to spay them while they're going through it."

"How much do you charge the city?"

"The put-down fee? Five bucks."

"So, is she worth ten dollars alive, or five dollars dead?" Billy almost smiled. There was something straightfoward that he liked about the freckle-faced girl.

"That depends entirely on you. I have two small boys. I can't be adopting any cats."

"All I've got is a five-dollar bill," Billy said. "Can I pay you the rest when I pick her up?"

"We can handle that." The brown-haired girl glanced up at him. Alert brown eyes with a smile behind them. "What's her name? If we're going to keep her, we need to put a name on her cage."

The image of Mrs. Stamforth's thickly-powdered face brought to mind a great-aunt of Billy's. "Clothilde. Her name's Clothilde."

"Spell it for me?"

"*Cee. Ell. Oh.* Oh, what the heck. Just call her Tildy."

Billy had gotten a registered letter from a law firm in Omaha. It contained instructions for him to claim a disbursement from the estate of Clothilde V. Franklin Dixon, of North 14th Street, Lincoln, Nebraska. The old woman had died without a will, and the law firm was tasked with dividing up her property according to a formula which was spelled out in the letter. His share, one thirty-second, was a fraction of a surprisingly large amount. Billy ran the numbers and calculated his cousin Ruth's share to be exactly four times his. It was enough to buy herself a new Chevy. Which she did.

GERARD HORSE LOOKING'S trial for the murder of his sister was to begin the following Monday. Gerard had been released from the hospital to the county jail. He had not spoken of his sister or her death; in fact, he would not speak at all. The community of Turtle Lodge looked forward to his conviction with an enthusiasm out of proportion to its regard for the teenaged girl. Alive, Bernadette had been a challenge and an embarrassment, reluctant to attend school and refusing to sit quietly when she went. In death, she became a victim robed in innocence. Her funeral was crowded with men and women named Sorenstam and Battersea and Schmidt, who cried hot tears as if she'd been one of their own. They buried her below the frost in the McDonough family plot near the town of Haines, with the red coat she wore when she died folded at her feet. The other coat, the one Billy had bought her as a sort of consolation prize, still hung in his closet.

The bayonet that killed Bernadette Horse Looking remained at George Smith's truck barn, where Billy had hidden it under the seat of a used-out truck. The absence of a murder weapon troubled the county attorney, a great balloon of a man who could barely get up the courthouse stairs. To prepare for the trial, he questioned Billy over and over about what he had seen in the alley behind the Pleasant Hour. Billy had the answers pat, but lest they seem too well-rehearsed, he introduced some uncertainty. "How near was the defendant to the victim when you found him? How many steps?" "I don't remember. I guess between ten and thirty." He understood he was to be the primary witness, and he got a fresh haircut and made sure that his uniform was pressed.

Nobody in Turtle Lodge doubted that Gerard had killed his sister except for the husband of Billy's cousin Ruth. George Smith saw grounds to disagree with his wife on any subject.

The dead girl in question continued to plague Billy with hallucinations. He never knew where or when she would appear. Usually it was the living room of his house, where a streak of her blood had fallen. There'd been a braided rug, which he'd burned, but blood and liquid had soaked through the rug and into the floor. He spent much of his spare time scrubbing it, but the floor had not been waxed in a long time and the grain of the porous wood had absorbed the stain.

"What are you doing?" Her voice came from behind him. Billy didn't look around.

"I'm trying to get this blood up."

"That blood is mine. You need to leave it there to remind you of what you did." Bernadette stepped around him, to stand between him and the door, holding the red coat tight around her waist. Her feet left bloody tracks on the oak flooring. "You think you can make my brother take the blame," she said, "but I won't let you."

"What are you going to do, testify before the jury?" Billy wiped up the fresh footprints that she'd left. The pink scrub water seeped between the floorboards.

"I might. Who's going to stop me? You?"

"I'm the only living person who can see you," Billy pointed out.

"That's what you think. I bet they'd listen to me if I showed them *this*." She opened her coat, as she always did sooner or later. Her inner parts drooped obscenely from the slash in her belly.

Billy sighed. "Cover yourself," he said. "You've made your point."

"And my point is?"

"That I shouldn't have fought you for the bayonet? That I should've let you go ahead and stab me?"

"How about this: maybe you shouldn't feel so relieved to be rid of me."

"But I am not rid of you," Billy said. "As we see."

Some nights she let him sleep. Other nights he felt an ice-cold leg thrown over him and woke up cursing the wallpaper. The night before the trial she left him alone, but it didn't help. He dreamed that he was walking through a field of roses, but that the petals of every bloom he picked turned to blood in his hands.

BILLY ARRIVED AT the courthouse early. Prospective jurors waited outside the locked doors, huddled into their coats, the fog of their collective breath visible against the floodlights. A car with Omaha license plates had taken the parking space nearest the entrance; there were also cars with plates from Lincoln and Norfolk. One man carried a Speed Graphic camera on a strap across his shoulder. Billy went in the side entrance using his special key and climbed the wide, squeaking staircase to the third floor. The building was ice cold, the heat just coming on and clanging the ancient radiators, and he remembered his job in Lincoln, getting up at four to stoke the boiler of his high school. Whoever was in charge of stoking this one was a little slow.

There was a special room for witnesses—more like a closet—and the bailiff was already on hand to usher him to it. Billy was not supposed to see any of the jurors before the trial, lest he say something that might prejudice them. A box held a few old *National Geographic* magazines, and he passed the time by looking at pictures of African women's breasts. There was a lot of rustling and bustling out in the corridor, and the bailiff brought him coffee and carrot cake, but he had the feeling of being a stowaway, as if the courthouse was a ship whose crew and passengers were unaware of him.

Time passed, a lot of it. Billy guessed that the jurors were being questioned. The bailiff came in and walked him to the restroom. Billy wearied of looking at exposed nipples and read an article about seals. Then he read an article about Mardi Gras in Brazil. The women in the Brazil article were better-looking than the Africans. He supposed that they kept in shape by swimming. He had begun to read about the Amish who had settled in Mexico (nothing to look at there) when a great commotion started in the hallway: footsteps, voices, general outrage, the distant banging of a gavel. Nobody came in to tell him what it was about.

After a long time the bailiff entered, wiping his forehead with a blue bandanna. "Sorry, son," he said. "What with all the ruckus, I kind of forgot you."

"So is it time for me to testify?" Billy placed the magazine on a chair and rose to his feet.

"Testify? Oh, hell, no. You can go home now. The case is dismissed."

"Dismissed?" Billy felt the room begin to spin. "What do you mean, it's dismissed? It can't be dismissed."

"Well, yes, it can. Old Judge Brown declared a mistrial. Says there's not enough evidence to prosecute a skunk for stealing strawberries. Says without a witness or a murder weapon, this case ought never to have been brought to court."

"What about Gerard?"

"Released. Sheriff took him out the back way. As far as I know, he's a free Indian."

Billy put his hand to the wall. His knees felt wobbly. "But—"

"It's all right, bucko," the bailiff said with a knowing wink. "This town ain't through with him. You might still get your chance to testify. There's more than one way to skin a cat."

Billy tried to slink out past the treasurer's office, but his cousin Ruth caught him and pinned him to the wall. "You heard?" she hissed, her breath redolent of tobacco. "You're a man, or you pretend to be. What are you going to do about it?"

"Let me go," he whispered back. "Not now. I don't feel good."

"You and George. You're a pair to draw to." She raised her voice so that it echoed down the hallway. "*I am not anxious to walk down Main Street and meet another woman's murderer walking toward me. Just because some 80-year-old judge whose testes no longer function thinks a female's life has little value, that doesn't mean that justice cannot be served. If the law refuses to hold a criminal responsible, a community can take other action.*" A light patter of applause came from distant parts of the building.

"I'm on duty tonight," Billy said, blushing. "I might have to—"

"You don't have to do a God-damned thing," Ruth said. "Take a nap, or take a crap. Take a vacation." Before pivoting to return to her desk, she lowered a hand and, gently but emphatically, whacked him on the nuts.

NEAR THE FOOT of the courthouse steps, where the wind was blocked and the weak sun shone a little, men had gathered into groups. One group centered around Rudy McDonough, the relative-by-marriage who'd gotten Billy his constable job. A larger cluster had formed around a burly blond-haired rancher with a scarlet face and the neck of a bull. Otto Hudspeth. "The Hudspeths came to town for the trial," a man next to Billy said. "Now there's not going to be any trial, so they're saying they might stay for the hanging."

"There can't be a hanging without a trial," Billy said. "Besides, hanging isn't legal. The State of Nebraska uses the electric chair."

"You're not from around here, are you, son?"

Rudy McDonough motioned Billy to come and join his group. "Have you seen Gerard? We're concerned for his safety."

"I was told the sheriff took him," Billy said. "I didn't see them go out."

"It's not that we're sentimental," Rudy said. "It wouldn't look good for Turtle Lodge if something happened to him. A reporter from the *Omaha World-Herald* is standing with that other bunch right now."

Billy glanced across at the larger group. A ring of men had formed around Otto Hudspeth. Not all were ranchers or townspeople; a few wore shoes and expensive overcoats that labeled them as coming from the city. "Maybe we'd best stay out of it," a man at Billy's elbow said. "You know, let Starchy Sedgwick take care of it. Starchy knows how to handle those Hudspeths."

"He can't handle six or eight of them by himself," Rudy said. "Billy, what will you do? If anything happens, it'll happen tonight. That's your shift."

"I have no authority outside the city limits," Billy said. "So far, nobody's asked me to do anything." He backed away from the group and hurried toward his car. His intention was to shed his uniform as soon as possible. He'd gone to bed at three and had gotten up in time to get ready to testify. He planned to take his phone off the hook and try to sleep.

BECAUSE HE WORKED nights and slept mornings, Billy usually kept his shades drawn tight, so the front room of his house was dark when he opened the door. Before he could switch on a light, heavy arms embraced him and held him in a smothering grip. He tried reaching for his revolver, but a huge hand clamped his arm to his side. After a moment of panic, he realized that Gerard was being careful not to hurt him, and as he gradually relaxed, the other man relaxed, too. They stood there, uncertain as to what to do next, until Billy freed an arm and flipped the light switch. "Gerard? What the fuck, man? What are you doing in my house?" The giant Indian held a finger to his lips. His eyes went from Billy to the door. Billy turned and closed it. "Gerard, talk to me. Tell me what is going on here."

The other shook his head in the negative. He gestured with pursed lips toward the next-door trailer. "Somebody burned a cross in front of our trailer," Bernadette's voice said. "It was a shitty little half-assed cross, but my brother got the message." Billy glanced to his right. "He doesn't talk,"

Bernadette said. "He can't. I think something's broken inside his brain."

"I didn't know this town had KKK," Billy said.

"They've got everything here," Bernadette said. "Or if they don't, it doesn't take a lot of imagination." She stood there barefoot in her red coat. For once, she didn't seem intent on tormenting him. She clutched the red coat tightly and vanished.

Billy turned to Gerard, who was studying him with a puzzled look. "Do you want me to take you back to the jail?" he asked. "I could arrest you for something, you know, say you were trespassing."

Gerard shook his head in the negative. He didn't want jail. Billy cast about for something else he could suggest, but nothing came to him. Finally he said, "What about breakfast? I could eat some eggs and toast myself."

Gerard's eyes lit with interest, so Billy went into the kitchen and put a skillet on and broke some eggs into it. He got out a wire toast holder and inserted two slices of bread and held it over the burner. "I can never get this right," he said, "but it's better with eggs than just plain bread, don't you think?"

Soon he found himself eating breakfast with a man who should have been his enemy. Bernadette did not appear. Gerard finished his eggs and held his plate out for more. Billy turned the burner back on and broke four more eggs into the pan. "Didn't they feed you in that jail?"

"Nnn." The man could produce sound, anyway. He'd never been one for a lot of conversation.

A noisy pickup truck went by outside, then another. Their exhausts were not the typical ranch-truck drone, but the warble of tuned V8s with glass-packed mufflers. Gerard flinched. He evidently didn't feel the need to display bravado. "Hudspeths," Billy said. "They're watching your place, not mine."

Billy slid another plate of eggs in front of Gerard and got up and went into the front room. Bernadette stood there looking at him. "Any ideas?" he asked. "You seem able to get around without people noticing." She didn't speak, so he passed her and pried open the window blinds. The street looked normal. Flakes of frost glittered brightly in the February sun. The temperature remained well below freezing.

"The trouble is," Billy said aloud, "I don't have any friends to back me up." He let the blind snap shut and turned to face her. "I'm not going to do anything," he said. "I've done enough stupid stuff already." He went back to the kitchen and sat down again across from Gerard, though he avoided the big man's gaze.

"W-w-ww—"

"Who was I talking to just now? Nobody. A fig newton of my imagination."

He made more toast and got out a jar of apricot preserves. Billy knew Gerard had an appetite for sweets; he expected him to consume the entire jar, and that is what he did. The two men sat without talking. More vehicles went by outside. "I'm going to change out of my uniform now," Billy said finally. "I have to put it on again in a couple of hours, and I'd like to take a nap."

When he woke, Gerard was standing at the end of his bed, shaking his foot. There was the sound of a diesel truck engine idling. "M-man," Gerard said. "Door."

"Somebody's knocking," Billy said. "I hear it. Let me put my pants on."

The person at the door was George Smith, back early from Iowa or wherever he had been. "'Lo, Billy," he said, walking in without ceremony. "I've been listening out at the coffee shop. Sounds like they've got Gerard convicted without the benefit of a jury." He glanced toward the door behind Billy. "My wife is on the warpath. Just so you know. Hello, Gerard."

"Isn't she always?"

George Smith flushed a little darker and glanced at the floor. "Ruth's collaring every man who'll listen," he said. "She wants the town to get together for a necktie party. Says we're a bunch of pansy-livers. Says this is not the kind of behavior she expected when she moved west." He looked up at the two younger men and shrugged. "Who the hell knew what Ruth expected? Billy, maybe you could talk to her. She might listen better to a blood relative."

Billy recalled a recent blow to his testicles. His stomach knotted, and he glanced at Gerard. If the big Indian were to be lynched, it would be the end of any local investigation, but there might be a federal grand jury that would drag out awkward details. His own relationship with Bernadette might come to light, and that by itself would be a mark against him. "I don't want to talk to her," he said. "The woman despises me."

"It's a man's life at stake," Smith said. "This fellow—I don't know if he done anything or not. Whether or not he's guilty, he deserves a chance for a jury to decide, not a crowd of liquored-up dingbats. You're getting paid to be a lawman of some description, and you owe it to support the law. Seems to me it ain't too much to ask of you, just to talk to Ruth."

"What about him?" Billy glanced at Gerard. "I don't want him here, but he's got nowhere else to go. His trailer doesn't even lock."

"Tell you what," Smith said. "That tractor of mine has got a sleeper cab on it. He can crawl up in there, and if nobody sees him getting in, I expect he'll be all right until I can drop him off somewhere out in the plum thickets. How about it, Gerard?" Gerard lifted his huge shoulders and let them drop. "I believe I'd pee first," Smith said. "There's no bathroom in the sleeper. It could get to be a long cold afternoon."

Once the two men left his house, Billy expected Bernadette to show herself, but she did not. Even more than Bernadette's apparitions, the thought of confronting Ruth gave him the shivers. He remembered the kitten he'd adopted, or had meant to adopt—though it had only been a couple of days, it seemed like weeks had gone by since he'd left her at the vet's—and even though he didn't really want a pet, he changed his uniform pants for street clothes and went out again.

THE GIRL AT the veterinarian's office had a framed photo of identical two-year-olds on her desk. "Yup, those are my twins," she said. "Zeke and Earl. They're Hudspeths, more's the pity."

"So, you're married to a Hudspeth, then?"

"I divorced him. He's in the state pen in Lincoln. He got caught with a truckload of stolen cattle. They were his uncle's cattle, too. Dumb as rocks, but he did have a pretty way of sitting on a horse." She had a comical laugh; first her eyes would open wide, then air would pop from between her lips. Soft brown curly hair cut short. Long waist, broad shoulders.

"Were you in the barrel racing last summer?" Billy guessed by her erect posture and by her horsewoman's waist. He hadn't gone to the rodeo over in Haines.

"I didn't win, so I'm surprised you'd remember." She finished some bookwork and stood up to go fetch the cat. She came back out cradling the little animal against her breast. "She's still a woozy Suzie," she said. "We'll keep her again tonight, if that's OK with you."

Billy reached out to touch his kitten. Her nose was divided down the middle, half pink and half brown. He could feel the warmth of the girl's sweater on the back of his wrist. "That's fine," he said. "I'm not set up for her yet. Should I get a box of sand?"

"Get commercial cat litter from the grocery store. Line a cardboard box with newspaper. Cats love boxes. You'll need to change her litter twice a week."

"Should I buy her some milk? I don't drink any myself."

"Absolutely not. No cow's milk. Milk will make her sick. Get dry cat chow. If you want to give her a treat, offer her a bite of tuna fish."

"I don't know the first thing about cats."

"No worries." The girl showed him a grin that displayed a prominent diastema. "She'll train you."

"She couldn't be worse to deal with than two identical Hudspeths. A bunch of their relatives are in town right now, looking to make trouble."

"Oh, God." The girl mock-shuddered and gave a rueful smile. "After they told me it was two heartbeats, I cried for days."

It felt good to be on friendly terms with at least one person in Turtle Lodge. Fortified by his visit, Billy decided to find and confront his cousin. He didn't know what he would say to her; he didn't know whether he wanted Gerard lynched or not. But he felt bound to Ruth by the murder, more than ever. If Ruth hadn't gotten herself worked up about the coat, Bernadette might be giving him grief as a live girl rather than a dead one. By that logic, Ruth was implicated even though she was unaware of it. It was the strongest claim he'd ever had on her.

A WOMAN AT the treasurer's office informed him Ruth had left work early. Her car was not in the driveway of her house. Cruising Main Street, Billy spotted it in front of the Pendergast Hotel, and on a hunch he parked his slow little '49 Chevy and went into the tavern across the street. He found her sitting at the bar with her back to the rail, surrounded by ruddy-faced men wearing cowboy boots and jeans. They had light blond hair, dark necks, and heavy shoulders, and wore snap-button shirts tucked into belts that appeared to cut off circulation at the hips. He shoved his way through the crowd, not without drawing some appraising glances. "Ruth, I've got to talk to you."

"Well, look who's here." She gave him her sweetest smile. "The representative of the law as it exists in Dunlap County."

"Please cut the crap," he said when he got close to her. "What you're doing is going to get me fired from my job. I'm already skating on thin ice."

"How could it?" she asked. "You're taking the night off, aren't you? Can't you have an attack of vertigo? Something serious but not too frightening?"

"I'm supposed to keep things quiet around here tonight. You can see how that's working."

"Oh, poor you," she said. "No sweetheart and no job. You might have to pull up stakes and move to California."

"God damn it."

"Hey, is this guy bothering you?" one of the Hudspeths asked.

"He's my cousin," Ruth snapped. "He can bother me if he wants to." She turned back to Billy. "For a limited time only," she added quietly.

"About me and Bernadette," he said softly, "not everybody in town knows about it. I'd prefer to keep it that way, if you don't mind."

"Oh, you would, would you?" She gave him a speculative look. "There's no accounting for people's taste. Especially men's. Anyway, I don't see what your affair has to do with the drunken idiot who stabbed his own sister."

Billy had an inspiration. "Maybe I'd prefer to kill him myself."

Ruth glanced at him with a fleeting moment of respect. "You? Well, that's different," she said. "If only I believed you would do it."

"He beat me up once," Billy said. "I owe him for that already."

"Fine. Do you know where he is right now?"

Some change in Billy's expression made Ruth put down her drink. "What the hell," she said. "Something is going on here. You'd better tell me, because I'm going to find out anyway."

"Talk to your husband," Billy said, and turned to leave. On his way out, he noted the two newsmen from Omaha, sitting in a booth and nursing drinks. The photographer had his Speed Graphic at his side.

THE WESTERN AUTO store sold plastic pans for catching oil changes. Billy thought one of those would do better than a cardboard box. When he carried the pan and cat litter into his house, Bernadette put in her two cents' worth right away. "What's that, a catbox?" She was standing in the kitchen. "Who said we were getting a cat? I don't like cats."

"You'll like this one. She's pretty."

"I don't care how pretty she is. I don't want a cat."

"You know what?" Billy said. "You're dead. You don't get to decide." He knew that would not be the end of it, but when he glanced into the kitchen, Bernadette had gone.

A few minutes later, as he was getting into his uniform, she reappeared, standing at the foot of the bed. "About Gerard," she said, "what are you going to do?"

"Nothing," Billy said. "Gerard is not my problem. If they want to hang him, I'll let him hang, so long as they do it outside the city limits."

"Gerard is my brother," she said. "You'd better do something to help him, unless you want to be dealing with both of us. So far, you haven't exactly been a great friend to the Horse Looking family."

Billy tucked in his shirt, buttoned his uniform pants, and tightened his belt. "Hey, look at me," he said. "I've got my cop suit on. If you want something, call the dispatcher."

"You think I can't," Bernadette said. "You'd be surprised what I can do. Remember, whether you help him or don't help him, I'll be watching."

Billy strapped on his revolver and picked up his jacket off the bed. Before leaving, he turned back to grab his flashlight and gloves. "How far can you, uh—I mean—"

"You want to know if I'm a mental projection or if I exist independently, is that it?" Billy ducked his head and blushed. "I can go anywhere you go," she said. "I have other ways of traveling, but they're not as straightforward. Why do you ask?"

"Well, I—It's just that, if he hides or runs away, I might need help finding him." Billy rubbed his lip-suture with his knuckle. He could feel his mustache growing in. "Truthfully, there is little that I can do," he said. "When it was only the Chinese army, rat-a-tat-tat, no problem. But if it's the Hudspeths. . . ." He let his voice trail off. "Let me know if you think of something."

"There's that cheap crummy coat you bought me as a replacement," she said. "Take it to the Smiths' and hang it on a chair."

"How is that supposed to help me locate Gerard?"

"Just do it."

BILLY FUELED THE patrol car at a special locked compound that the city maintained at the base of the water tower. It required two keys, one for the padlock at the gate and another for the padlock on the fuel tank. One purpose of the compound was to keep the town's high-school boys from painting the year of their graduation on the tower; nevertheless, a fresh inscription appeared there every spring. A proposal had been made to build a second water tank atop the butte that overlooked the eastern edge of town. There were other ideas for using Turtle Lodge Butte, one in particular involving a TV relay tower, so that citizens could receive broadcasts from a station in Reliance, South Dakota. Nothing ever came of these proposals, not because of the difficulty of building a road to the top of the butte but because of rattlesnakes. The butte was so infested that hardly anyone went there. Sometimes Indians from the Rez used it for ceremonies; once or twice a year, drumming and chanting could be heard. No one knew exactly what they did up there.

February was the safest time of year to climb the butte. Billy wished he could go there and sit out the long cold night. The wind might be bitter, but maybe he could find a place where no ghost would bother him.

He locked the supply tank, drove the patrol car out and locked the gate, and settled behind the wheel for his night of patrolling. First he drove up Main Street to check on the number of pickup trucks. All three bars were busy, including Doug's, the most disreputable. He crossed the highway and circled the courthouse block past the county jail. (Turtle Lodge boasted two distinct lockups: the county jail for criminal suspects like Gerard, and the drunk-tank jail that ruined the basement of City Hall.) Starchy Sedgwick's personal car was parked beside the dispatcher's; the sheriff's patrol vehicle was not in evidence, which meant that Starchy was already out to try to keep a lid on the night's activities. Two state highway patrolmen lived in Turtle Lodge, but whether they had any interest in a local matter like a lynching, or whether they even knew one was imminent, Billy could not tell. Once he'd made a slow circuit of the town, he drove to the George Smith residence, with the unloved replacement coat on the seat beside him. Death was on Billy's mind as he approached the front door. He'd once had to try not to listen while a foxhole companion drowned in his own blood; the process had been slow and desperate, and Billy had hoped then that the blow when his own time came would be clean and abrupt.

He rapped at the aluminum screen that closed off the entry. George Smith opened the inner door and came down the shallow step to meet him, and Billy shoved the unwanted red coat toward him. "Hang this over a chair," he said.

"What?" Smith drew back as if the coat had blood on it.

"Take it." Billy racked his brain for an explanation. "It's damp. It needs to dry out. Hang it over a chair."

Smith took the coat and stepped closer. "Can you go out to the truck barn and check on my passenger? If he's still there, bring him over here. He hadn't ought to be left alone once it gets dark." Billy swallowed hard and nodded. "You might grab a burger to go," George Smith said. "I expect he hasn't had nothing."

Just then Ruth came storming through the inner door and down into the entry. She grabbed Smith's arm and shoved him to one side. "What's this?" she asked, staring down at the substitute coat. "I demand to know what is going on here."

"Um, I thought," said Billy. "I mean, you know, it might fit—"

"*If that coat belonged to who I think it belonged to*," Ruth shrilled, "*it's not coming in this house.*"

"Hey, it doesn't have cooties," Billy said. "It's almost a brand-new coat. There's nothing wrong with it."

"Well, take it to the Hospital Auxiliary then, or give it to the fucking Methodists to keep people fucking warm in fucking Africa. If you think I would ever wear a thing like that, you're crazier than George, here, and George is crazy as a fucking pet raccoon." She snatched up the coat from her husband and flung it at Billy. "Take it to that killer you're so fond of. Tell him it's from his sister."

"Gerard did not kill Bernadette," George Smith said. "I've explained it to you fifty times. Somebody killed her earlier and dumped her body in the alley. The doctor said she was stiff."

"*Frozen* stiff, you rustic moron. If Gerard didn't do it, then who the hell did? You don't suppose *I* did it, do you?"

"No," George Smith said. "I don't suppose that." The two of them glared at one another in a way, Billy realized, that he and Ruth never had. And never would, unless they ran off somewhere and got married.

He folded the orphan coat over his arm. "I'm going," he said. "If the two of you want to yell at one another, that's not a problem as long as you keep it inside the house."

"Go and fuck yourself, you insufferable piss-ant," Ruth said.

"It's cold out there," George Smith said. "Please drive safely."

BILLY KILLED TIME the way he always did, by patrolling the streets in a pattern: south on Main, turn left, down First, up Second past the school, down Third past the back side of the school, over to Fourth which was the east-west highway, in and out past idling semis parked and waiting in the Milestone's lot, then continuing west on Fourth and south on Main again. There were other parts of the town and other variations, but this was the slow orbit he traveled most. It took him past two of the three bars and past the movie theater, and he could glance to see what was going on at the Pleasant Hour and at Doug's, which was off on a side street. Every fourth circuit he drove the alleys on either side of Main; he would walk these same cold alleys at eleven o'clock, to test the locks on the back doors of all the businesses.

The sun went down, and the February wind got colder. When he judged it had gotten dark enough, Billy left his rotation and drove south past the edge of town, to where the big tin building housing Smith & Son Enterprises sat surrounded by dead weeds and piles of scrap iron. Yellow light shone from the windows and vapor rose from the vent, and a nondescript brown station wagon sat out front. Billy knew the wagon without looking at the license; it belonged to Smith's Negro mechanic, Albert Watson. He got out of the patrol car carrying his flashlight, then had second thoughts and tossed the flashlight back onto the seat before closing the door.

The steel building was wide enough to be the hangar for a small airplane, and in fact that is what it had once been. The customer entrance beside the big roll-up door swung inward. Billy opened it to see two tractors sitting in tandem, both with sleeper cabs; the one in front was idling, with a flex pipe through the roof to suck away the exhaust. The air inside the barn was warm but unpleasantly fumey. Watson was over at the workbench, filing at a piece of metal he had clamped in a vise. "Hey," said Billy, closing the entrance door behind him. "Stinks in here."

"Hey," said Watson, putting aside the file. "What's up?"

"George sent me over. I'm supposed to pick up somebody."

"Not me, I hope." Watson went over to the welder and took a sip from a can of beer that was sitting there. "I haven't been doing anything illegal, if you don't count playing poker."

The cab of the idling truck squeaked, and a rustling came from within. The passenger-side door swung open and Gerard stuck his head out. "B-Bill," he said. "Bill-lee."

Watson put down the can of beer and moved back over to the vise. "I don't know anything about this business," he said. "I didn't even know he was in there."

95

"Relax," Billy said. "We're all on the same side here." *Anyway, for the time being*, he added silently.

Gerard climbed down from the truck and offered Billy a handshake. Billy gripped the giant's soft hand and studied its deformed fingers. He couldn't meet the big man's look. "I'm here to take you to George's house," he said. "He thinks you'll be safer over there. That is, if Ruth doesn't shoot you. I was supposed to bring you a hamburger, but I forgot."

"I got him a burger," Watson put in. "It's me that George is concerned about. Doesn't want me anywhere near—" He made sure that Gerard was looking at Billy and lifted a closed fist to the side of his head, giving an upward jerk. "I didn't go along with him on that; I think Gerard's better off staying here. But George is the boss."

"He's not my boss," Billy said. "I'm just here to give a man a ride."

"Guess I can shut that diesel off now," Watson said. "Stinks in here."

Gerard wasn't dressed for the cold; he had only a sweatshirt. Billy held the patrol car's door for him. "That coat on the seat is your sister's," he said. "It won't fit you, but you can wear it across your shoulders." He went around to the driver's side and slid halfway in before his rear end encountered the flashlight. He placed it on the seat between them. "Tell me something, Gerard," Billy said. "Do you remember anything at all about the night Bernadette was killed?"

Gerard looked down at the flashlight and rubbed the bridge of his nose. He turned to stare out the window. "Nn-nn," he said.

"I don't remember it too well myself," Billy said. "It all happened in a blur. That was a terrible thing."

They rode to the Smiths' house in silence. Billy pulled up to the curb, stopped the car, and went around to let Gerard out. "This isn't going to be pleasant," he said quietly. "Ruth's got a hair up her butt. Earlier today she was in the bar trying to organize a posse to hang you." Gerard paused and glanced up and down the empty street. "I think you'd better go in," Billy said. "I can't take you to the jail. That's the first place they'd look."

Gerard, wearing the substitute coat over his shoulders, lurched up and out of the patrol car and toward the entry, stumbling as he ran. Billy followed, taking his time. Whether Gerard got hung or got away, suspicion would follow him; as long as Gerard was suspected, he, Billy, would remain in the clear.

When George Smith answered Billy's knock, he had the expression of a man who hears the first shots of a battle. Ruth was right behind him. She stepped back when she saw Billy and Gerard in the entryway. "Oh, God," she said, "I *knew* this was coming."

"It's just for tonight," Smith said to her. "Do you want them to hang an innocent man?"

"Hang *him?* Yes, I want it," she said. "I want to see his broken body dragged behind a pickup truck." Billy caught the unfocused look in her green eyes; something chemical was clouding her vision, something from the extensive pharmacy that filled her bathroom cabinet.

"Well, I'm keeping him overnight," George Smith said, "and that's all there is to it."

"*Not!*" she said, and ran to the telephone. Smith did not try to stop her. She picked up the receiver and rattled the cradle. "Operator," she said. "Operator, there's a murderer in my house. Do something." She slammed it down. "There," she said. "I've called the police."

"*The police* is your cousin here. He's standing in the door with his mouth open." George Smith shot a disgusted glance toward Billy. "What you've done just now is to let everybody else in town know where Gerard is at."

"Well, I'm glad," Ruth said. "I hope they hang all three of you." Near the kitchen end of the living-and-dining rooms, there was a vestibule off to one side that led to the couple's bedroom and the bath. Ruth ran and disappeared there, slamming a door. After a moment, another door slammed and they heard the clacking of an old-fashioned latch.

"She's took over the bathroom," George Smith said. "It's the only door that locks."

The three men passed through the living-and-dining area and pushed through the swinging door into the kitchen, where there were three plain chairs around three sides of a dinette table. A window looked out into the back yard. Propped against the window frame was George Smith's hunting rifle, a Model 1903 Springfield from the First World War. "Have a seat, fellows," Smith said. "I'd break out the whiskey, but I'm on guard duty." Gerard took off Bernadette's spare red coat and hung it on the chair opposite Smith.

"I'm not staying," Billy said. "I can't. It's my shift. I have to patrol."

"I understand that," Smith said. "You might drive by this place once in a while. I'll leave the front door open so you can see what's happening."

Billy turned to go. "Sit down, Gerard," Smith said. "I'll fix you something to eat. Do you like sardines?"

"Nn," Gerard said. Billy left them there. When he looked back from the street, he could see straight through to the kitchen: Smith on one side, Gerard's broad shoulders, and then the substitute coat on the third chair opposite. The rifle propped against the window frame was also visible.

A parade of cars and pickup trucks rolled up and down the Smiths' street until past midnight; Billy joined the procession in his patrol car, eyes straight ahead. Starchy Sedgwick sat in his sheriff's car down the block, on the opposite side of the street. A light stayed on in the bathroom of the Smith house, and there was also a light in the spare room next to the entry. The couple's bedroom and the boy's room remained dark, and Billy concluded, correctly, that Ruth was spending the night in the bathroom, that Gerard was asleep in their son's room, and that the boy was using the spare room at the front, where he had his schoolbooks and radio. George Smith sat alone at the kitchen table, smoking cigarettes and playing solitaire.

There was talk in the town later that a few of the drivers-by had seen a long-haired Indian girl in a tomato-red coat, seated across the table from Smith. Whether it was that, or the Springfield rifle, or Starchy just down the street, no one tried to enter the house that night.

The sun came up to find George Smith and Gerard Horse Looking gone. Smith returned in the evening as usual, having taken a load of steers to Iowa, but Gerard was not with him. That day was the day Ruth Smith left town for good. The man who pumped gas at the Milestone said she headed west. Among the things she left behind: a double-barreled Fulton 28-gauge quail gun; her electric sewing machine; photographs and papers from her decade in Turtle Lodge; and one tall, confused, and angry ten-year-old son.

THE VETERINARIAN'S OFFICE girl met Billy with a smile. She gave him a pink collar and a tag engraved with the name *Tildy* in cursive script. "Happy Valentine's," she said. "She's an indoor kitty now. She wants to look nice for you." She set the cat on the counter and put the collar on her. The cat lifted a hind foot to scratch at it, but other than that she did not seem troubled. She sniffed Billy's hand and rubbed her forehead against his sleeve. "Look at that," said the girl. "She's putting her mark on you."

Billy paid the additional five dollars. The cat sniffed his billfold. She had short unlovely gray-brown fur, faintly rippled with caramel. Her white feet added charm to her step. He could feel the bump of each vertebra in her tail. "Hello, Tildy," he said. "You're going to come live with me." She looked up at where his voice had come from, stepped toward him, and rubbed her small forehead against his shirt.

After Billy had brought his cat home, he wondered if he should have named her "Trouble." She tore through the house, first in one direction and then another, the patter of her feet a welcome racket in the empty rooms. She seemed to know what the catbox was for, but other than her tidy bathroom habits, she created chaos wherever she went. She unballed his socks, pulled dish towels off the rack, and spun the toilet paper roll like a Vegas slot machine. She even found a way into the attic and clattered around up there. She had a way of dropping off into a doze from the most violent activity. After he came home from work at two and went to bed, she would fall asleep in the middle of his back.

Billy bought her every cat toy the dime store carried: a soft rubber ball, a catnip mouse with a bell on it, a dyed feather at the end of a string. She preferred pens and bottle caps. He tried teaching her to retrieve the ball, but she would only bat it until it rolled underneath a chair. He spent more time looking for it than she did. He spoiled her and petted her and even gave her a little cream, in spite of the veterinarian girl's instructions. She lapped it up greedily and came down with a spectacular diarrhea.

"Told you," said the girl at the vet's office. "No cow's milk."

"But I've seen cats drink it," Billy protested. "My uncle's barn cats north of Lincoln practically live on cow's milk."

"Cats like that have gotten used to it," the girl said. "You can let her lick ice cream off your finger. Just a tiny bit, though."

"I get it. No cow's milk. Are you going anywhere for Easter?"

"Just to my in-laws' ranch. They deserve to see their grandkids once in a while. The boys will run wild like the little thugs they are."

"Will you do any riding while you're there?"

"I will not. I don't ride horses with those people."

To make up for the extra hours in December—Billy had received no holiday time at Christmas; it was his job to keep citizens from smashing into one another, and though Turtle Lodge had limited traffic, any car on the streets during the holidays after ten p.m. was likely to be traveling a crooked path—the city clerk gave him one night off in March. It fell on a Tuesday, and Billy drove to the veterinarian's office and asked the desk girl out for a movie. She said it would be all right if she could drive. He glanced out the front window at a surplus military Jeep with a canvas top. "That thing?"

"That way I know there'll be no hanky-panky. Those seats make love impossible."

Billy gave his house an extra cleaning and bought a rug to cover the bare subfloor in the living room. The kitten dug her claws in and rumpled the rug, then hid beneath the mountain range she'd created. Only her bony whip of a tail showed. "I hate that cat," a girl's voice said at Billy's shoulder. "That cat looks straight through me."

"You're back," Billy said to Bernadette. "I thought you'd cleared out. I haven't seen you since Gerard left."

"Why are you cleaning and sweeping? Do you have a date?"

"I do, as a matter of fact," Billy said. "Does that make you angry?"

"Why should it make me angry? I don't own you."

Billy pondered this for a second and felt his throat constrict. "No, I guess you don't," he said hoarsely. "If anybody owns me, it's that damned Ruth, and she's left town."

"Maybe you should've killed Ruth instead of me."

"I keep telling you," Billy said, "that whole thing was a mistake."

BILLY THOUGHT ABOUT canceling his date—if he was still high-centered on Ruth, there was little reason to proceed—but the girl's freckles and frank brown eyes reappeared in his mind. *Friendly*; the veterinarian's office girl was *friendly*. In the years since his pretty cousin taught him the ropes, he'd usually been able to get sex, but he had to think back to his sister Irma to discover a female friend.

If they wanted, they could sit through a double feature: *Thunder Over the Plains*, with Randolph Scott, and *Abbott and Costello Go to Mars*.

Weeks of below-zero temperatures had frozen fire hydrants and split the boles of trees, but on Tuesday the cold gave way to a sultry thirty-six degrees. Gray slush trickled in the gutters. Billy took the opportunity to use ammonia to clean the windows of his house. He polished both sides of the glass until they sparkled. Then he noticed Tildy was missing. While he'd cleaned the glass he'd left the front door open, and of course the half-wild cat had gotten out. Until then, he'd been able to keep her inside.

"Here, kitty. Here, kitty kitty kitty." He couldn't manage the high cat-calling voice. He searched around his foundation and under the Horse Lookings' trailer. The neighbors opposite had a shed and a giant woodpile (his own small house was heated by an oil stove) but he knew that, because he was a cop, they would not welcome him poking around. He went back inside and left the door propped open. The town took up less than a mile from east to west, and barely half of that from north to south; if Tildy failed to come in, he would find her if she lived, but he worried that a dog might grab her. Loose dogs roamed the run-down neighborhood south of the railroad, and coyotes howled at night at the edge of town.

Around five, the temperature dropped below freezing, and he gave up washing windows and watching for Tildy to come in. He took a hot soak in the tub and put on clean clothes. At six he made himself supper, salmon patties with onions. His cat did not come crying for salmon scraps. Billy wiped his dishes and stared gloomily out the kitchen window. The streetlights were coming on. With the door open, the living room was chilly, even though he'd turned the stove up high. He did not feel he ought to leave it like that while he and the brown-haired girl went to a picture show.

"You're upset about that cat." Bernadette. "I told you we didn't need a cat."

"Good grief! Can't you give it a rest? She's a skinny little thing and she's probably scared."

"I was thin. I was scared. Did you worry this much about me when I went out at night?"

"I worried plenty. There's no cause for you to be jealous."

He heard the purr of an approaching motor, a four-cylinder Jeep by the sound of it. A gust of wind blew the door closed. There was a woman's cry in the street outside and the scrape of rough tires on gravel. Billy put down the dish towel, feeling sick at his stomach, and went to the door and looked out. The veterinarian's office girl was stooping to lift something off the street.

She came up the step to meet him with tears on her cheeks. She held the dead kitten in her arms. "Somebody ran in front of me," she said. "It looked like she came from your house. She was wearing a red coat."

"Nobody came from here," Billy said. He reached to touch the bloody, brindled fur. "It's not your fault. You tried to miss her."

The girl snuffled. "I can't go out with you," she said. "This side of town gives me the creeps." She wore a buckskin coat with fringes; she'd put on rouge and perfume.

"I understand. Let me see if I can find a box for her." He'd put snakeskin around a cigar box to make a jewel case, but that had gone to Ruth. He went inside and found a cardboard shoebox, lined with soft paper.

The girl placed the limp cat in the box and wiped her cheek with her wrist. "Ah, well," she said. "She's not the first dead kitty I've held."

"I'm sorry it happened," Billy said. "It's my fault for letting her out."

The girl snuffled again and turned away. Tildy's blood had ruined her coat. "I guess I'll go and pick up my kids," she said.

"Maybe another time?" The air brought a whiff of her scent. It was pleasant and clean.

"I don't think so," she said. "I'll be seeing you around."

"OK, right," he said with his hand on the jamb. "I'll be seeing you." She left him standing with a weighted shoebox. The night that had fallen seemed already too long. His house was cold, but the windows were clean.

It took two hours the next morning to chip a hole in the frozen ground with a spud bar he borrowed from the McDonoughs' garage. He retrieved the substitute coat from the Smith house—nobody there was going to wear it—and wrapped the shoebox in it and stuffed it in the hole. That night he went on patrol the same as always. He beat the first drunk he arrested and broke the kid's wrist with his flashlight. Luckily for Billy, the twerp was from Willow and had no important relatives.

Mercy

THE PATROL CAR lurched as the left front tire rode up and over the softness of a human body. Billy Dixon opened his eyes wide and slammed his boot down hard on the brake pedal, and the '50 Ford screeched to a halt. Dead and wounded Chinese soldiers carpeted Main Street as far north as the highway. One of George Smith's cattle trucks rolled up behind him; the airbrakes squonked. The driver tapped the air horn, twice. The truck's giant grille filled his rear-view mirror.

Boop boop! Billy's fists remained locked to the steering wheel. It was a warm June evening, with the daylight-saving-time sun still high and yellow. Though he drove with the window open, a bead of sweat made its slow way down his jaw. Fred Jackson, one of Smith's drivers, came up to the window. "You OK, bud?"

Billy blinked, and the bodies disappeared. "I'm all right," he said, easing his grip on the wheel. He glanced at Jackson's sleeve. The man's left arm ended in an L-shaped hook, the hand lost somewhere in the South Pacific. "Does that hand bother you?"

"Funny time to ask," the trucker said. "I'll tell you about it some night when we're not blocking traffic."

I've got to get more sleep. Billy put the car in gear and continued patrolling. Since December when the bayonet killed his lover, the year had cycled back around toward summer, and though nothing particular had happened to him—anyway not since the case against Gerard Horse Looking got dismissed—he had gone to see the doctor because of his nerves. The doctor prescribed black-and-yellow capsules as fat as bees. "I used to love those," Bernadette told him. "They made me feel mellow, like whiskey."

"They don't do a thing for me," Billy said, "and I wish your mother would leave."

"Throw her out," Bernadette said. "You're the big cop with the sunglasses." She still left bloody footprints around the house, and he had to mop the floor three times a day. So far, the mailman hadn't seen her, and nobody else came to his door. She hadn't quite driven him crazy, but he didn't know how much longer his mind could withstand her intrusions.

AFTER THE KITTEN he'd adopted got squashed, Billy showed no mercy toward stray animals. If somebody in Turtle Lodge complained about a stray, he took the creature to the dump and shot it. He bought aviator sunglasses and grew a thin mustache, and he never smiled without a tinge of sarcasm. He'd received two shocks in February that changed his life. The first was when Judge Abe Brown declared a mistrial in the Horse Looking case. The second came the following day, when his beautiful cousin Ruth left town forever.

Money that arrived from his great-aunt Clothilde's estate paid off the mortgage on his house, with enough left over to buy the Horse Lookings' trailer and a couple hundred dollars besides. He had just concluded the trailer purchase—the owner was John Iley of Ileyville—when an Indian woman whom he did not know moved in without his permission. This woman was real, alive, and breathing, but she proved as hard to get rid of as Bernadette. She wouldn't look at him or speak to him. "That's the way with Lakota mothers-in-law," Bernadette explained. "You're supposed to ignore each other."

"Mothers-in-law? You and I were never married."

"She thinks we were," Bernadette said. "It doesn't take a lot to count as marriage on the Rez."

Bernadette's mother bought a brand-new mattress and planted it in the front yard amid the dandelions. She bounced on the springs and shouted out to strangers, in English and in Lakota. On warm clear nights when the coyotes south of town were calling, she turned up the radio and sang along with Patsy Cline in a voice that scraped like a truck unloading gravel. She started arguments with broken-down cowboys and yipped at the moon. "Jesus Christ," Billy said to Bernadette, one dry-mouth morning after the racket had kept him awake. "Is *that* what you would've turned out like?"

"Who knows? We aren't going to find out."

Of course, the woman was Gerard's mother, too. Gerard Horse Looking had left Turtle Lodge after he'd barely escaped being lynched the night of the mistrial. People said that he'd gone to Sioux City, that that was where George Smith had taken him. There was no telling where he might have gone after that. Not to know Gerard's location made Billy antsy, since Gerard was now his enemy if he only knew it.

The mother's name was Rose. Rose looked to be in her late 30s and was dark of skin. She stayed in shape by jumping and dancing on her mattress, and she looked fit and attractive for as long as she kept her mouth shut. She quacked like a duck in a voice meant to scare away bears. Billy feared her chopped-off hair that bristled with electricity; when she went off on one of her atomic binges, she radiated a manic energy that gave him goosebumps. Billy could see that sooner or later he'd be called upon to lock her up.

He heard about a cop opening in the next town up the road, but if he took that job, he would have to sell his house. It was reassuring to own a house, even if Bernadette came with it. The only pleasure he got from his current job was making Indians miserable, and that would not improve if he moved one county west. He longed to lie on Mrs. Althea Dodson's sofa cushions and contemplate his future as a screen actor, but that daydream phase of his life in Turtle Lodge had passed.

Billy dreamed almost every night that he was back in Korea. These images persisted into his waking hours, so that when he saw an Indian family on the street—or, sometimes, just a group of black-haired children—Asian faces would crowd his patrol car's windshield and his free hand would drift to his revolver. Other nights he dreamed that the population of Turtle Lodge had formed a posse to hang him. When the mob turned the corner carrying shotguns and a noose, his long-legged cousin Ruth led the pack.

Meantime, he and Bernadette dwelt as do many thousands of couples, in the comfort of a bitter silence and a cold, cold bed.

IF A DAY happened to be sunny, Billy might run the steep trail to the top of Turtle Lodge Butte. He liked to look for the rattlesnake den that everybody said was there. The view from the butte was a soft green vista. Grass-covered hills rolled away southward like the sea, dotted here and there with groves that were the shelterbelts of ranches. The shadows of puffball clouds raced across the land. If he looked east, he could see the water tower of the next town, but far to the west, the horizon was clear.

In Pleistocene times, the butte had been an island in the channel of a broad but shallow river, one that had retreated northward along with the glacier it fronted until it followed approximately the path of the present-day Missouri. Buffalo seven feet high at the shoulder, with horns as wide as a man's extended arms, roamed its banks in herds that numbered in the millions. There'd been horses no bigger than deer, hairy rhinos, camels the size of antelopes and antelopes the size of camels. It was a world watched over by cranes and eagles and ruled by lions and giant wolves and bears. Logic told him that the wind coming off the glacier would have had a witch's bite in summer and would have brought pure arctic misery in winter, but when he looked down and envisioned that lost channel, with its sunny braided gravel bars yellow-bright with willows, he longed to be able to walk there among the reeds. Best of all, there'd have been no thirsty little town at the foot of the butte.

Bernadette's mother Rose (she didn't answer to Horse Looking; someone suggested to Billy that her name might be Stevens) was not the only person below the butte on whom he felt he needed to keep an eye. George Smith kept arguing at the café that Gerard hadn't killed his sister, at least not in the alley where she was found, that the knife could not have simply vanished, that her body would not have had enough time to freeze. Then there was Ruth's son, who always looked too long at him. Starchy Sedgwick, the county sheriff, wanted Billy fired for incompetence, and his boss the city clerk called him "that moron." The card players whom he flashlight-taxed always met him with tightened lips, and it was for certain that the Indians didn't like him. Even Althea Dodson, the pharmacist's wife, looked askance at him since he'd quit screwing her. He found it particularly galling that the pin-boys at the Pleasant Hour laughed at him, because Jonesey, the daytime constable, was popular with them. All that sorry individual ever did was chew gum and write parking tickets. Balls of Wrigley's Spearmint, wadded in their wrappers, appeared nightly in the ash tray of the patrol car.

Billy got his hair cut every Tuesday morning, and while he waited in the town's only barbershop, he paged through outdoor magazines. Though he caught rattlesnakes and skinned them, he had no taste for hunting, but he was fascinated by photographs of custom target rifles; he liked the way their gunstocks flared into smooth voluptuous curves that cradled and caressed the shooter's cheek. Billy was no shooter—he'd been made a machine-gunner in the Marines because he couldn't hit a rifle target—but he pictured himself as a sniper, holding off an army of Communists from the top of Turtle Lodge Butte. If the Chinese invaded, he could be a hero, a defender. Men would look up to him.

Along with its other lines of business, the Pleasant Hour Lanes and Tables sold sporting goods. A locked cabinet held shotguns and rifles for sale, new and used, but none were target rifles. Billy told the owner that, if such a rifle did come in, he would like to fire it.

Billy woke from his midday nap to the sound of someone pounding on his door. He scrambled out of bed thinking that this must be his occasion, his time to step in and take charge, to show Ruth and the rest of the townspeople his essential character. But as he reached the door in his underwear, he remembered that the town was hollow, that his lovely red-haired cousin had been gone for months.

The creator of the disturbance was Rose, the crazy woman from the trailer. "Hey!" she shouted as if the door remained closed between them. "Big flashlight man! *Wasichu*! Snake Ass!"

"What do you want?" Billy said evenly. It was the first time she'd addressed him face to face.

"Take me to my daughter."

He glanced back over his shoulder to see if Bernadette was in evidence.

"What you looking at? Nothing back there. Take me to my daughter grave."

"All right. Let me put some pants on." He left her on the step and went back into the bedroom, where Bernadette stood watch near the foot of the bed.

"Don't let her get in the car with you. My mother is dangerous."

"Your mother is a pain in the ass. What harm can she do me?"

"You don't know her," Bernadette said. "Bad Pipe women can't be trusted. They're vengeful and can set the spirits against you."

Billy did not believe in spirits, but he slipped a blackjack into his pocket, just in case. They took his private car, a droning six-cylinder Chevy, and he drove a bit under the speed limit, west toward the dying town of Haines, Nebraska. The woman beside him thumped her foot on the floorboard and hummed something from the Grand Ole Opry. Her body gave off a smell like the ashes of a campfire.

The two McDonough families owned a burial plot in the graveyard east of Haines, a plot that, like the town, stood mostly empty. Rather than let Bernadette go nameless into a pauper's grave, they had buried her with their people, at the end most distant from Rudy and Baldwin's parents. Baldwin McDonough said it was a waste of money, but Ellen McDonough, his sister-in-law, had been adamant. She herself had a child buried there, a stillborn baby girl; where a lilac bush shaded a small white stone, there were a few leaf-blades of irises. Ellen McDonough bore the same relation to Billy as did her sister Ruth, so her baby would have been his relative, though he seldom thought of it.

Barbed wire fenced the cemetery, but an iron gate stood open. Bernadette's bare-earth mound was not hard to find. She had no stone as yet, though Ellen had plans for one. Billy shut off the senile Chevy's motor, and a meadowlark's trill floated in the window. "Here it is."

"This her? My little girl?" The woman looked at the grave mound. "Shit."

"They had a nice funeral for her. The Methodists took care of it."

"Nobody told me."

"They didn't know how to contact you. Gerard was in a coma."

"I never seen her hardly since she was a baby. Her grandma raised her. I never wanted kids. I never would've started with men if I knew there'd be kids." The woman looked at him as if she expected sympathy. "Don't you hate kids? I do."

"There's one kid I hate," Billy said. "The rest I don't think about."

"Well, so that's my daughter, and she's dead," the woman said, gazing at the mound. She made no move to exit the car. In Lincoln, Nebraska, where Billy had grown up, cemeteries were green, the soft grass weeded and kept trimmed. In this dry cemetery, the buffalo-grass sod hid a minefield of tiny cactuses. Dark-green sunflowers pushed up here and there, their flower heads undeveloped. Somebody, probably Ellen, had made a visit to clear windblown trash from the family's grave markers.

"Shit," the woman said again.

"Any others, besides this one and Gerard?"

"Hell, no! That big stupid Gerard baby ruined my hole. This girl, she so tiny I thought I'm having a turd."

Billy felt his neck redden. "We should have brought flowers."

"I don't care about that," the woman said. "Let the weeds grow. Weeds got flowers. What say you and me go have a drink?"

"No, thanks," Billy said. "We have to get back. My shift starts at four."

"All you white-boy cops got a cob up your ass. Why the fuck is that?"

They drove the ten miles to Turtle Lodge in silence. She had him drop her off in the alley in back of Doug's, where there was a shelter made of two-by-fours and rusted tin, with the remains of a picnic table and a couple of folding chairs. "Looks homey," Billy said. "I'll be collecting drunks later, so watch yourself."

"Any cop picks me up tonight is going to have his hands full. I thank you for the ride."

THE LONG TWILIGHT had ended; black night curled above the streetlights like a she-wolf guarding her pups. Bernadette's mother pivoted on the center stripe of Main Street, giving the finger to teenage drivers who swerved to miss her. Billy rubbed his hand across his cheek and stopped the patrol car. "Get in."

"Fuck you, big cop bastard. You can't make me do nothing."

"I can make you," Billy said. "Get in, unless you want to try on chain-link bracelets."

She opened the rear door on the passenger side. "You are a poop head," she said. "You spoiling my fun."

"That's my job," he said. "Did you have a pleasant evening?"

"You better shut up," she said. "I'm not done with you yet."

He took her to the basement of the city hall, where there were four cells in a row, each nine by seven feet with two narrow iron bedsteads bolted to the wall. He put her into the first cell, then woke the residents of the second cell and moved them to the third. They were two men similarly dressed, wearing cowboy boots and jeans and snap-button shirts. They both smelled of Old Spice and vomit. One had straight black hair and dark-brown skin, the other red curly hair and freckles. "I like that curly-headed one," she said. "Put me in the cell with him."

"Female company, gentlemen," Billy said. "Behave yourselves."

He hung a privacy blanket over the top bunk of the empty cell and went back out to prowl for additional customers. The town was quiet, and around twelve-thirty he had coffee at the Milestone before returning to make a last check. He found the woman naked; she had somehow reached out with her toes and torn down the blanket. The two male drunks sat side by side on the lower bunk of their cell, heads lowered, hands propping their foreheads and covering their eyes.

"These two geniuses aren't no good," she said, turning her nude self to Billy. "I can't even get 'em to look at me. What about you?"

"Put your clothes on," Billy said, "or I'll turn the hose on you."

"Hey, great," she said. "Hose me. Hose me all you want."

Billy reached past the bars to strangle her and shut off her noise, but her nipples caught his thumbs' attention and his palms found her breasts. They were warm and full of life and brown, the dark skin tender. She looked up at him, and her eyes softened. "Put your belt around my ass and lift me up," she said. "I ain't as young as you."

AFTER SHE'D BARKED out a love-cry in her harsh tobacco voice, after they'd backed away from one another, she said, "Coppy, you done me a favor. Now I'll do you one. Look up when you go outside. Them people up there on the Spirit Road, that's your relatives, your *tiospae.*"

He did look up just before he went to bed, standing in front of his own dark house and afraid of what he might hear from Bernadette. But there were no faces above him in the night sky. He saw only the watery jizm of the Milky Way, splashed across the stars.

The Spirit Road; that's what Rose had meant. He knew that much about Lakota culture.

"That's right." Bernadette stood beside him. "You fucked my mother."

"How do I even know she's your mother? You people are full of lies."

"You shouldn't have done that," Bernadette said. "The wrong things

110

you do down here will catch up to you on that road and hold you back."

"If that's your road, why don't you get on it? Take your mother with you."

"I will, when people here release me."

"I'm not holding you. I'll be glad to have my house to myself."

"You are holding me, and the house is mine as much as yours."

In fact, the house was mostly blank. No potted plants in the windows, hardly any furniture. A stucco box with a roof, set squarely in the middle of a corner lot. From the street, it was hard to tell if anyone lived there. Gerard's broken trailer, with its filthy mattress and weeds, looked more alive.

The Faces

BERNADETTE HORSE LOOKING'S mother left town on the Rapid City bus, and for a while it looked as if she'd taken her murdered daughter with her. After a week with no ghost in his house and no noise next door, Billy Dixon crossed his yard to investigate. The weather had turned hot, and the aluminum door and window frames sealed the Horse Lookings' trailer as tight as a coffin. The air inside reeked of stale incense and ammonia. Fly corpses and Sterno cans littered the floor. A five-gallon bucket of shit stood in the bathtub, and cigarette burns dotted the linoleum. Billy hauled the ruined mattress to the dump and scraped away the crust from the kitchen counter, put out poison for the rats and cleaned away every trace of the woman except her smell. She had evidently burned sage in every room. All his cleaning and discarding left the trailer uninhabitable, but he'd bought it mostly for the privilege of tidying up the lot. He fumigated with DDT and hung fly-strips from the feed store, and left it all to broil in the heat of the sun.

With no madwoman next door and no chill presence in his bed, Billy ought to have enjoyed untroubled sleep. Instead, each morning after he got off work at two, he watched an impossible river of faces stream before him. These were not the blurred images of memory—his mother's face or Ruth's would have softened in the mind's damp mirror—but faces razor-sharp as photographs from *Look* magazine, stark, superreal, of both sexes and of every race and age, each face engraved with its individual, unique story. They might appear singly at first, but then they'd arrive in clusters, then in swarms. Morning after morning, he came home and laid his weary body down, only to have a whole State Fair crowd jostle to observe him. They stared the way kids stare at a carnival show's freak.

The faces didn't belong to anybody he knew, and there didn't seem to be any repeats. It stretched credulity that the human mind—in particular his own, which he'd always thought to be limited—could generate such an avalanche of detail. One hot July night Billy gave up trying to sleep and dragged himself out of bed. As he stared down into his coffee cup, wishing for a thunderstorm to break the humidity, a familiar voice spoke from across the table. "My mother has been sending them," Bernadette said. "They're people who died today."

"All right. Could she please send them somewhere else? I don't need your mother conducting tour groups through my head."

"You should see the doctor. You could get us some more of those black-and-yellow pills."

He raised his cup and sniffed the coffee steam. "I feel great, except for my nerves," he said. "Welcome back, by the way," he said to the empty air. The girl had vanished.

Bad mornings notwithstanding, Billy looked confident and strong in his brand-new uniform. He bought it with his own money, since the city clerk wouldn't pay for one, and because he ordered it from the catalog himself, he got an officer's stripe down the outsides of his pant legs. He had it tailored to fit; he still kept his body trim, even though his cousin Ruth had stepped out of his life forever and his visits to Althea Dodson had ceased.

Billy watched the night baseball games when the town was quiet and no misbehaviors required his attention. Growing up in Belmont, on the northwest side of Lincoln, he had played no baseball, though there were pastures nearby and plenty of boys around. His mother always put in a two-and-a-half acre garden, and he'd hoed weeds in the heat and slaved to carry water in buckets. By contrast, each summer until Labor Day when school began, his cousin Ruth's son played baseball every afternoon. Billy visualized tossing the little turd a live grenade, the orange-red flash and the boy's corpse holding forth the stump of a shattered arm.

THE REPUBLICAN PRESIDENT, Dwight D. Eisenhower, lifted the ban on selling alcohol to Native Americans, and repercussions quickly arrived in Turtle Lodge. Dodson the pharmacist no longer made extended trips to South Dakota, and he canceled his order for a Cadillac Coupe de Ville and bought a Chevy station wagon off the dealer's lot. The Indian population dropped by half, as happened in other Nebraska towns along the South Dakota border.

With the Indians mostly gone, Billy didn't make enough arrests. The city clerk grumbled. "Some asshole is setting fires," he said. "Junk piles, trash cans, crap like that. Probably the same kid who was blowing up people's mailboxes around the Fourth."

"I'm aware," Billy said. "I have an idea who's responsible."

"Congratulations. Everybody knows it's the Smith boy doing it. Maybe you could give him a talking-to. You're his uncle or something, are you not?"

"I'm not the right person to do that," Billy said. "I don't like the kid or his father, and they don't like me."

"George has a lot on his plate since Ruth left." The clerk sighed. "I need you to stop the little jerkoff before he burns somebody's house down. Catch him in the act and kick his butt for him. Justify your salary."

Billy began keeping tabs on his cousin Ruth's son. Every weekday after suppertime, the stork-legged bully ran the neighborhoods at the head of a mismatched following of boys. Later, at the end of twilight, when other kids his age had been called inside, he would go back out to prowl the vacant lots and alleys. He made use of the streetlights' shadows, so that it was seldom possible to tail him. Even so, Billy came to know his territory—boys had their territories, like tomcats—and he felt it was a matter of time until he made an arrest.

Had Ruth still been around, there would naturally be hell to pay, but Ruth had taken a job in faraway Seattle. If catching Ruth's son might be a way to re-connect, the truth was, Billy couldn't imagine it. When he tried to recall those lost and sacred times, he found that his heart had grown scar tissue. One day while he was probing to test that bone-deep ache, he heard a voice say, *Ruth, schmooth. What do you want with that sour pickle?* If it had come from Bernadette, he would've expected it, but the voice was his own.

IN AUGUST, AS goldfinches appeared among the sunflowers, a new music teacher arrived in Turtle Lodge. One evening when the downtown stores stayed open—it would have been a Thursday or a Saturday—Billy spotted her as she window-shopped. Her hair was redder than his cousin's, and she was at least a decade older, but he could see that she'd been as striking a woman as Ruth. Six feet tall at minimum, she wore high heels to shop; she parted the crowd with the impatient stride of a racehorse. Rumor had it that Baldwin McDonough had already gotten to her.

"One more horny white bitch. Just what this town needs." Bernadette no longer confined herself to the house. She haunted the city's patrol car on nights when she felt closed-in.

"You don't need to talk about her," Billy said. "She doesn't know anybody. Who do you think is supposed to tell her that Baldwin is a philandering shit?"

"Poor cop boy. You're already in love with her red hair. I've got news for you. It's dyed."

"I feel sorry for her, that's all. You know how these people turn vicious when somebody slips."

A target rifle with scope had come into the Pleasant Hour. Billy bought it and began teaching himself to shoot. When he removed his shirt and gazed into the mirror, he saw a mark of honor, the yellowish bruise of a gunstock just inside his shoulder.

Baseball ended and the high-school football games began. There was the usual flurry of tickets issued to 16-year-old drivers. Frost collapsed all the squash vines and killed the tomatoes, so that the backyard gardens smelled like garbage and had a desolate look. Halloween came upon Billy with a warning from the city clerk. "Kids here are used to getting away with pranks. Your mission is to show yourself, but don't get too involved. You pick up the wrong kid, I could lose my job. Remember, the election is Tuesday."

"Are there kids I *should* pick up?"

"Probably not. Halloween is a north-side thing. The little greasers from your side of the tracks tend to not cross over."

With his ears still warm from the city clerk's advice, Billy fueled up the patrol car for a night's cruise. He put six fresh batteries in his flashlight and dusted off his old ill-fitting uniform so his tailored one wouldn't get damaged in a scuffle. He hoped the night might offer him a chance to catch Ruth's kid in some kind of outlawed trickery. He made sandwiches for later and ate a late lunch or early supper.

His shift began at the parking lot of the congregational church, where he watched from across the street as parents dropped their pre-teens off or ushered their costumed toddlers to the door. The sky was still light and the first star not yet visible, the fingernail moon a sliver in the mauve west. He kept an eye on the entrance but saw no sign of Ruth's boy. Parental traffic tapered off and he heard high voices inside the church, singing *today's the day the teddy bears have their piiiic niiiic.* Billy put the patrol car in gear, drove half a block south, turned east on Second, crossed Main, and continued past the school, but the bouncy tune and lyrics remained in his head.

"So this is the night all the ghosts come out," Bernadette said. "Big whoop tee doo."

Billy glanced to his right, grateful for the distraction. "It's the Celtic New Year," he said, to remind her that he was a man who read things. Bernadette was either fully present or she was not. She was never some wisp of mist you could thrust your hand through.

"For us, it's time to find a relative who's got a stove and a pile of firewood," she said. "It's no fun sleeping on frozen ground."

"Do you sleep? Where do you go when I'm not seeing you?" Billy was curious about the lives of the dead, so to speak. But when he glanced toward the passenger seat again, his lover was gone.

Billy drove south on Main and out of his jurisdiction, passing the city limits sign and Smith & Son's truck barn at the edge of town. All the lights at Smith & Son were on, and the mechanic Watson's car was parked outside. He continued south another mile to the next country intersection. As he turned around to come back north, a pair of headlights swung into the truck barn's driveway, and when he came abreast again, George Smith's straight-eight Buick—"old George's old gray mare," Ruth had called it—was parked there. The wheel-less truck cab where Billy had hid the bayonet sat among dead stalks of horseweeds. A year's worth of rust would have accumulated on the blade. He suffered an urge to take the thing from its hiding place and soak the dried blood off and polish it.

Turtle Lodge City Limit, Pop. 1876. The year of Custer. Billy spent at least six hours out of every twenty-four driving, driving, and driving, but the patrol car was never supposed to pass the city limits sign. So far, Billy had only violated that rule by a mile or two.

Halloween happened to fall on a Sunday that year, but some businesses in town had a car parked in front and a light turned on inside: the Ford and Chevy dealers, a beauty shop, a closed café, a tavern. Billy wasn't getting paid overtime—he ought to have had Sunday off, since the bars were closed—but the city clerk said he could have a comp day later in the year.

He drove up the alley behind the music teacher's house. The music teacher left her Nash out on the street, so the space behind her garage was overgrown and empty. Besides the Nash, the woman owned a witless Irish setter; its doghouse, also empty, sat two-thirds back in the lot. He supposed she would be keeping her dog inside. Billy felt no special warmth toward dogs. His work took him into unfenced yards and empty lots, where he stepped in more than his share of dog poop.

The weedy space behind the woman's garage would just allow the patrol car to squeeze in. Her man of few secrets, bald-headed Baldwin McDonough, would be home on the range with his home-at-the-kitchen-range wife. Billy had had no sexual outlet since he'd stopped visiting Althea Dodson, who he assumed would be spending Halloween with her scrawny husband. Billy pictured a monkey rolling pumpkins up a steep incline.

The parking area next to the Milestone looked the same as any other Sunday night: a cross-country semi, some coffee-loafers' pickups, a couple of smoothed-off cars belonging to high-school punks. Billy drove the gravel loop behind the building, where the trash bin's pungent seepage overflowed. A cat jumped down and ran across his path. Somewhere in town, high-school seniors had their heads together, and the juniors, the next class following them, would be cooking up a rival stunt. Until their plans bore fruit, he had nothing to do but drive: left on Main Street, left on First; up Second, down Third; left on Pine Street, left again on the highway; left on Main. Pint-sized trick-or-treaters toddled down the sidewalks ahead of their parents, but the older cadre were still corralled at the Congregational church.

He drove up the music teacher's alley one more time. Salmon was the woman's name; Mrs., but no Mr. Her number wasn't listed in the phone book. Rotary phone dials had not yet come to Turtle Lodge; an operator sat in a brick building the size of a garage and connected each call manually. If he asked the switchboard operator to connect him to the music teacher, the operator might tell the world that he'd tried to reach her. Operators were known to eavesdrop and pass gossip, so the townspeople spoke with discretion over the phone.

There'd be no one to eavesdrop if he called the night telephone operator, but that unlucky female had a brown-edged overbite and a chest as lush and inviting as a box of Wheaties.

THE CONGREGATIONAL TRICK-OR-TREATERS, their bellies packed with cookies and cider, were loosed upon the town at eight p.m. Billy watched them swarm out of the fellowship hall in their costumes. A small gorilla and a large eagle, or something with a beak and feathers, got into banker Sorenstam's Pontiac station wagon. A kid in a purchased devil's suit took the passenger seat up front, and a long-legged boy with the beginning of a pair of shoulders stepped quickly from the shadows to join them. Ruth's son, dressed as a pirate, carried some type of steel hook tucked up his coat sleeve, most likely a bale hook. Billy started the patrol car's engine.

Rosemary Sorenstam, the banker's pretty wife, drove the station wagon. Billy bird-dogged her to a newer subdivision called Nob Hill, a neighborhood north of the highway where ranch-style homes sheathed part way up in brick sat at angles on sprawling lots, some on cul-de-sacs, some on streets that meandered for no reason. Rosie's wagon entered one of the cul-de-sacs and pulled into a broad driveway, and Billy followed at a distance and parked where he could watch them go in. After only a couple of minutes, five costumed tricksters came out—an extra kid must have been there waiting—and Billy followed their progress without getting out of the car. ("Nob Hill" was a local sarcasm, since the subdivision was platted on land as flat as a lake.) First one dog would bark, then another, then he would glimpse them through the hedges. The smallest of the five, the one in the devil's suit, led the way.

Trick-or-treating, like baseball, was something Billy hadn't taken part in; his father, who ruled with his fist, equated it with begging. Even so, Billy saw that the spacious neighborhood was not optimal, and he guessed his little gang would soon cross the highway. When he saw the knot of them heading south, he put the patrol car in gear and crossed over, maintaining a one-block separation. Here, the houses sat together in compact rows; many more kids were out with their wheedling cries and masks. He lost track of the five, but he felt confident he could pick up their trail later, once the chill settled in and the younger goblins went home. In the shadows of a rusting fuel depot by the railroad tracks, Billy parked and ate his sandwiches.

As he put away his lunch box, a stray thought popped into his head. Out of nowhere it suddenly occurred to him to play a prank on the music teacher. He knew how to set up a field telephone, and he had parts of the apparatus lying in an unused bedroom. He would tap into her phone line, call her up, and disconnect. Then she and the hollow-chested telephone operator could go nuts trying to figure out who'd called.

From the fuel depot it was two blocks to his house. He scouted his back room full of military castoffs and quickly assembled all the parts. The field telephone looked like a prop from a war movie: a heavy wooden box with a crank sticking from the top and a receiver left over from the 1930s. Its wires ended in alligator clips. He lacked a set of batteries, but the patrol car's 6-volt system would do the trick, and he was expert at jumping wires, having had early schooling from his car-thief relatives. Billy loaded his apparatus into the trunk of the patrol car and re-crossed the railroad tracks toward the school.

He knew that Bernadette was watching him, but she made no comment.

Cars other than his patrol car were now out cruising. He recognized a new Chevy belonging to the son of the town's dentist, and an Olds driven by the granddaughter of the Milestone's owner. Both cars were crammed full of teenagers. While packs of mid-sized trick-or-treaters still roamed the town on foot, the high-schoolers drove their circuit and bided their time. Billy parked on Main with his headlights facing outward and waited for the moon to go down. Whatever the pimplefaces got up to, he figured he could do it better. Obsessed and pining for Ruth, then dropping out and joining the Marines, he'd missed out on all the fun of high school. Of course, kids in Lincoln did not envision the small-town weirdness that took place every Halloween in Turtle Lodge.

Billy felt like a kid himself with his secret phone.

OVERHEAD WIRES, BOTH telephone and electric, ran up and down the alleys of Turtle Lodge. Billy traced the phone cable from Mrs. Salmon's house back to its pole. He shinnied up, glad he'd worn his spare uniform, and attached the field telephone's clips and slid back down again. Next step was to connect the apparatus to the patrol car's battery. It had to be hooked up and tested in the dark because his six-cell flashlight had a beam that would blister paint, and he hadn't thought to bring along a smaller one.

After he'd wired it all together with modest damage to his knuckles, he gave the crank a spin and heard the telephone jingle inside her house. He felt a prickle of eagerness but did not wait for an answer. That would come later. He unclipped the wires from the patrol car's battery and left the crank box on the ground—nobody would be driving that alley in the dark of the moon—and closed the hood and went back to patrolling. A number of teen-driven vehicles circulated through the town and past the school, where floodlights bathed the apron in front of the building.

The patrol car's lights picked up five runners crossing First Street. They'd been over on the south side, bumming his cross-tracks neighbors for cheap treats. Billy turned the corner, killed his headlights, and drove around the block to follow them. A kid who was not a pirate split off from the group, and the four remaining entered a narrow house that faced the tracks. Lights went on, then off again, in a room up under the gables, and the four re-emerged, two of them without their candy. From there he followed them to the Smith house, where three of them waited in the chilly air outside. Ruth's kid went in and came out wearing a parka. He had ditched the hook. The four passed under the school's floodlights and turned east, then north, then east, pausing to knock at a couple of darkened houses. They rounded a corner and started down the music teacher's street, stopping to huddle beside her Nash parked at the curb.

After a conference that included some shoulder-shoving, the tall boy in the hooded coat broke free. Ruth's son went up to knock on Mrs. Salmon's door. He was turning to signal to his gang when the door opened and an arm reached out and snatched him in off the step. The door slammed to, and the light went off quick as a thought. Watching Ruth's kid vanish, just like that, made Billy's gut wrench. He took a deep breath and switched on his headlights and flicked the brights, and the remaining boys, who were about to egg the Nash, pocketed their ammunition and slouched on down the street. He idled up next to them and leaned across to roll down the passenger's-side window.

"You three shits get in the car. It's time you went home."

Billy stepped out and held the rear door for them; he made all three sit in back so as not to crowd Bernadette. As he got behind the wheel again, he glanced toward the empty passenger seat. *Show them your bleeding girl-guts. Give them a Halloween to remember.* Then he thought, *No, don't.*

He delivered them safe to their houses—the twins in their homemade costumes to the crackerbox on First Street, the kid in a Sears-bought devil suit to the Sorenstams'—and made a sweep to be sure the streets were clear of pre-teen foot traffic. He then circled back past the music teacher's house. Her lights were still on inside, but the porch light was off. He drove part way around the block to the alley's entrance, killed the patrol car's headlights, and entered the alley, stopping behind her house where he'd left his telephone rig.

Billy felt a fierce desire to know what was going on inside the house. He'd already made a phone connection, but the connection didn't work as a tap; he couldn't hear unless she picked up the receiver. Anyway, to eavesdrop was not the point. He'd only wanted to trick her a little bit. He thought he'd wait to hook it up again until after Ruth's kid had left. That way, when he called, he'd have her full attention. The local newspaper had warned its readers to keep their pets indoors; the woman owned an Irish setter so old and feeble that it wobbled on its legs. Her pathetic dog must be inside.

A light came on in a back room. Billy's heart thudded in his chest as a vision leapt to his mind of himself at thirteen, exchanging glances with Ruth and then sneaking off for sex. Only this time, rather than longing, he felt revulsion. If *that* was what they were up to, he'd put a stop to it. He got out and closed the car door quietly, and stepped across the low board fence. He felt exhilarated and nauseous, as in Korea in the foggy night when the shrill flutes played and the bugles blew and each man counted his ammunition.

With elaborate caution he approached the back of the house. Frost had stilled the air. The little wheel in the electric meter turned. He soft-footed it to the lighted window and looked in. Evidently the room was used for storage because it had no bed, only a dresser and some suitcases and cardboard trunks. There was nobody present. The pounding in his chest let up, but he still felt a tightness in his crotch and a copper taste on the sides and back of his tongue. Now he had to know what was going on in the front room. In passing, he peeked in the kitchen window. The music teacher was stirring cocoa in a pan. Her spoon left a splatter on the counter when she put it down. A bottle of gin stood open on the counter between the stove and the refrigerator.

Low voices came from the street out front; Billy tiptoed past the kitchen for a look. Teenagers had parked their cars at the end of the block and had slipped down to gather around the music teacher's Nash. Here was trickery he was supposed to be on the lookout for, but his patrol car sat in the alley next to a jury-rigged telephone. He couldn't rush out and scatter them, because they might circle back and find it. The knit collar of his leather jacket scratched his neck. The leather creaked when he moved to ease the itch.

The son of a man who ran the local livestock auction unlocked the Nash with a coat hanger and got inside to steer. The remaining boys pushed the little car past the front of the house, loose gravel cracking beneath the wheels. Billy slunk to the kitchen window to gauge the music teacher's reaction, but she'd taken the cup of cocoa into the front room. He could hear her and Ruth's boy talking; their voices sounded as if they were sitting on a sofa side by side.

Car engines started at the upper end of the block. Billy had to know what was going on in the living room. When he was sure the teenagers' cars had passed, he stepped across the dog fence at the side of the house and peeked around the front corner. The boys had pushed the Nash to the end of the block and were steering it in the direction of the school. He supposed they would get her car up onto the apron. The city clerk would ask him where he'd been, and he would have no answer.

So be it.

The living-room curtains were parted half an inch. Billy waited until the street was empty and slipped along the front of the house to peer in. What he saw there made him draw back with a hiss. A wall of strangers' faces gaped at him. It was his falling-asleep nightmare, come to haunt his waking hours. He dropped to his knees, panting, and closed his eyes.

Look again.

These faces were different. Their eyes were not alive. He shook his head to clear it. The faces were there, all right, twelve feet away and actual, but black-and-white, two-dimensional, not moving, frozen in time. Bernadette's cold lips pressed against his ear. "They're photographs."

Opposite the front window, in back of where the boy and woman sat, rows of framed studio portraits obscured the flower-dotted wallpaper. Unlike the faces that came to forestall his sleep, they did not stream or crowd past one another, and they were smiling. It was a collection of glossy photos of the kind that Hollywood actors mailed as souvenirs.

The music teacher and the boy sat apart and fully clothed. She was showing him an album of ships and planes.

Shaken and wrung out, Billy turned and walked back to his patrol car, scarcely knowing whether he made a noise or not. Bernadette had to help him disconnect the wires, and his arms shook when he lifted the crank box to set it in the car. He felt tears start when he thought of what he was letting the teenagers get away with. "It'll be all over town," he complained. "They'll say I was drunk."

"Not drunk," Bernadette predicted. "They'll say you were with *her*."

"That old dried-up has-been?" Billy would have liked to slap her, but his arms felt limp as seaweed. "I'll tell you one thing," he said. "She'd better leave that kid alone."

"I thought you hated him."

"I do hate him, I hate him a lot, and you and your witch of a mother can both go to hell."

"Hell won't take us," she said. "Hell's for white people. Hell won't let us in."

Justice

Lost. Lost. Lost. Lost. Billy Dixon's heart pounded so hard that it rustled the pillow's fabric. Only it sounded more like *cuffs, cuffs, cuffs, cuffs.* Bernadette next to him shifted her weight, which seemed to be increasing. "So what if somebody found your stupid bayonet," her voice said. "Go to sleep."

"How am I supposed to sleep with a dead person talking?"

"You're lucky it's only me. If all the murdered Indians talked, your ears would break."

Before the bayonet killed her, it had gotten bent when Baldwin McDonough ran over it with his pickup truck. That incident preyed on Billy's mind. A knife with a bent blade had to be unusual; most knife blades would snap. Baldwin, who owned a forge and knew steel, had turned it over in his hand more than once. The handle had a clumsy, awkward shape, the guard forked to clip around the barrel of a Russian carbine. Now the bayonet had vanished from its hiding place. Not fatal so long as it stayed vanished; but if it surfaced and became an item at the coffee drinkers' forum, Baldwin might recall that oddly-shaped handle.

"I'm not listening," Billy said to Bernadette. "What happened to you was a fluke. I don't deserve the electric chair."

"Don't trouble yourself," she said. "The worst that can happen is you'll get to see your relatives. You know I was a bad little Indian girl. Nobody but another Indian gets the chair for killing one of those."

"I come from good Belmont people. It's those Havelock Dixons who keep ending up in prison."

"They are all your relatives," Bernadette said. She had an unfair means of closing out an argument; she would simply disappear. Which she now did.

The previous winter, on Christmas Eve, Billy caught his cousin Ruth's delinquent son in the music teacher's back yard. The boy had set fire to her doghouse and burned up her dog. He said he didn't mean it, but he'd poured on half a gallon of gasoline; the jug was right there, and he had matches in his pocket. They held a court hearing in February, and Judge Abe Brown turned him loose. *Closer supervision.* He was ordered to report to the social worker twice a month. The person picked to supervise him was Mrs. Salmon, the music teacher. That made no sense to Billy. If one were to go by the gin bottles in her trash, the correct thing for her to supervise should have been a distillery.

When he made the mistake of complaining to Bernadette, she snorted. (If a dead girl snorted, could she fart as well? These matters preoccupied him lately.) "Justice! Don't come crying around to *me*. If you want justice, go see the sheriff and turn yourself in."

Turtle Lodge's light-skinned Negro, Albert Watson, kept a clean apartment above the feed store; Billy had gone there once, to collect his flashlight tax from the workmen's poker game. Watson worked as a mechanic at the Ford garage, but in the evenings and on weekends he maintained George Smith's trucks.

One spring day it had occurred to Billy that he might pin Bernadette's murder on Albert Watson. The bayonet that had killed her was already in place, under the seat of a junked-out cab at Smith & Son's truck barn. There would still be the Baldwin McDonough problem—seeing a bent blade in the local news might jog his memory—but Baldwin could be silenced with a rifle bullet. However, that would involve covering up a second murder, and it was clear from Billy's reading of detective fiction that murders-to-cover-up-murders became cumbersome. Even so, the thought that he could place the blame on Watson came to him like air to a drowning sailor. There were plenty of people in Turtle Lodge who would believe the worst of a black man. Baldwin might remember the blade, but he might not be credited. He consumed enough Old Yellowstone to pickle the cerebrum of a normal person.

Around Easter, this brainstorm of Billy's had become moot when he went to check on the bayonet and found it missing. It had not fallen to the floor or out the door of the cab; he made as thorough a search as he had time for. Naturally he suspected his cousin Ruth Smith's boy, but Albert Watson or George Smith could have found it. What made him lie awake at night was this, that after the previous year's mistrial, the bayonet's finder should have proclaimed its discovery. Billy couldn't fathom it. Some person in the community had to be playing cat-and-mouse with him. George Smith might do that. Ruth's husband disliked Billy, and he had his reasons. Another one who had it in for Billy was Starchy Sedgwick, the county sheriff. But if the sheriff had found the bayonet, he surely would've asked the public for information. There would've been a write-up in the *Thunderhead*: "Sheriff Reopens Horse Looking Case: Possible Murder Weapon Found."

Evidently, whoever found it was waiting for him to crack. *If I were going to crack*, Billy thought—head down and lip pushed out—*I'd have done it before now.*

Could Bernadette's brother Gerard have found it? Gerard Horse Looking had been seen in Dunlap County. Since the mistrial, Gerard had no outstanding warrants. There was nothing Billy could do about Gerard except to keep in practice with his target rifle.

After liquor became legal on the reservation, most Indians moved back north to South Dakota. Billy's work as night constable became the dullest police job in Nebraska. To keep from going crazy, he took to making late-night phone calls. He got to be an expert at connecting his portable telephone rig; he could hook it up, make a call, and be gone in ninety seconds. When he perv-called the music teacher, she laughed at him, but there were plenty of single women who were not so brazen. One woman had called the dispatcher before Billy could disconnect, and when the dispatcher got him on the radio, the result was a feedback howl that blasted through the patrol car's speaker. The screech was loud enough to rattle windows, but the woman inside the house had not caught on. That was the only time he came near to being discovered.

"If you want to fight crime in a place like Turtle Lodge, sometimes you have to commit it yourself," he said one night when Bernadette heaped scorn on him.

"Oh, please. No tough-guy jokes. John Wayne doesn't scare old ladies. At least not in the movies."

In April, banker Sorenstam flew his fast little Beechcraft into the ground. It happened out near the airport, so the sheriff got the call, not Billy. It turned out that Matt Sorenstam had fallen behind in a cattle-futures scheme, but the two life-insurance investigators who drove out from Grinnell, Iowa, could find no evidence that would sway Judge Brown, and the insurance company had to pay the bank (but not Rosemary) a quarter of a million dollars. Billy thrilled to imagine getting away with a quarter of a million. *You can't take it with you,* so the saying went, but Matt Sorenstam's business trips to Omaha and Council Bluffs had been greyhound-track-and-strip-club trips. He had taken it with him. Matt Sorenstam's pretty widow started work as a cashier at the bank.

Rosie Sorenstam became Billy's favorite midnight-phone-call target. If Bernadette said anything, he flicked sperm at her.

The snakes came out on Turtle Lodge Butte.

IN THE AFTERNOONS, before he went on shift, Billy took his sniper rifle to the base of the butte, where deer poachers had set up a firing range. He overcame his tendency to flinch and could hit a paper target at 500 yards, though he couldn't always put his round in the black. Farther out, at 750 and a thousand, he was not consistent enough to guarantee a kill. He bought surplus military ammo from an outfit in Missouri. It had to be shipped by train because the Postal Service refused to handle it, more evidence, if any were needed, of the U. S. government's turn toward the pink. Meanwhile the humdrum days went on. His immediate concern was the lost bayonet. Ruth's son did not appear to have it. Billy watched from a distance as the kid made friends with a new boy in town, the son of Jack Keogh, the man who took over the bank. Jack Keogh was a person of interest to Billy because he was a student of Communism. He wrote letters to the local newspaper praising Joseph McCarthy and warning of the "fifth column." Billy planned to ingratiate himself with Jack Keogh when he could, but so far he'd not had the opportunity.

His Baldwin McDonough problem almost got solved. Billy had his personal car towed to the Chevy dealer's because the gearshift lever stuck between two gears. Baldwin happened to be getting a motor mount replaced, and his pickup sat unattended with the hood up. When nobody was looking, Billy leaned in under the hood. The return spring that closed the throttle caught his eye, and he slipped a pair of pliers off the bench and crimped the spring wire where it wouldn't show. If the spring broke at the right moment, the gas pedal would fall to the floor and the throttle would fly open. The engine would then speed up uncontrollably.

The throttle spring did break two weeks later, but by some bizarre chance, the person driving happened to be Mrs. Salmon. The music teacher wiped out six cars on Main Street and put herself in the hospital. It caused a lot of talk and made an end to the affair between the music teacher and Baldwin, but none of the gossip touched Billy.

BERNADETTE WAS CHANGING. Her face had become rounder and less childlike, and she no longer tracked blood everywhere. She had less to say to him. She seemed to be thinking of something else.

"Why are you so quiet?" Billy asked her one morning. "Did you forget about making me crazy?"

"It isn't my fault if you're crazy," she said. "Let's hike to the top of Turtle Lodge Butte. I want to show you something."

"I'm not going up there with you." Billy thought to change the subject. "Your brother is around," he said. "One of the pin-boys ran into him out at Baxter's Pond."

"I know where he is," she said. "Stay away from Gerard. I don't want the two of you killing one another."

"I never tried to kill him," Billy said. "I only wanted to bloody his nose a little."

"Not true. If you'd been allowed to put him in a cell, you'd have beaten him to death with your flashlight."

"I'm not going to waste time arguing with you. It's the bayonet that worries me."

"Stop thinking about that bayonet. Come up on the butte with me."

"No."

128

MRS. SALMON FLUBBED THE SPRING musical by being drunk. She lurched up on stage afterward, barely able to navigate, and let the entire school board see her condition. A few days later, some railroad workers rescued her from the water out at Baxter's Pond. She had broken her leg. Two boys were with her, Ruth's kid and Jack Keogh's son, along with Albert Watson, the mechanic. The incident happened outside Billy's jurisdiction. He heard it from the dispatcher when he clocked in.

"Starchy's handling it," the dispatcher said, after she had sketched in a few of the details. "I don't think Starchy needs your help."

"What's to investigate? A drunk woman jumped off the railroad trestle."

"They're saying that her car might be down there under the water."

"A car in the water? That's ridiculous." A coil of dripping nylon rope lay in the corner of the dispatcher's office, with a good-sized horseshoe magnet tied to the end. "What's that?"

"Starchy brought it in. I don't know a thing about it." The dispatcher spoke without looking at him, and suddenly Billy's knees went wobbly. *Damp rope. Magnet. Boys on the railroad trestle. Somebody had been fishing for steel in the water of Baxter's Pond.* Hair stood up on the back of Billy's neck.

The next morning, he saw George Smith's Buick come into town from the south with an aluminum boat and trailer tied on behind. Starchy Sedgwick followed. Billy came near to panic then. He was packing to leave when Bernadette spoke to him. "Steady, mister," she said. "Don't run away just yet. Wait and see how it all plays out."

"How else can it play out? If they've found that bayonet, I'm done for."

"Maybe not. Anyhow your path is here with me."

"Path!" Billy tossed a high-school chemistry textbook on the bed. "There is no path. Do you know what Brownian movement is? It's the random vibration of particles. We're particles, bumping into one another. There's no sense to it."

"Explain my being here as random particles."

"My mind is disintegrating and giving off vibrations. You're a vibration."

Bernadette snatched a glass and threw it against the wall, where it smashed into a hundred splinters. "That glass just bumped into something," she said. "Sweep up those random particles."

"You're scaring me," Billy said. "It's time you left."

"You're right that it's time I left," she said, "but you don't know what you're asking."

He swept up the shards and unpacked his suitcase. He told himself that he'd postponed his departure, that he was staying because he wanted to, not because he had to.

When the music teacher and the mechanic, one white, one black, left town together, it outraged Billy Dixon as much as anybody. *That is what socialism leads to, a mixing of the races*, he repeated. Then a voice from another part of his brain replied, *What bullshit*. In practical terms, their running off was a godsend, since few would now defend Watson should Billy try to frame him. As for the mixing of races, there were men in Turtle Lodge who were known to maintain two families, one white and one half-Indian. In general, they were not shunned. People made a joke of it.

Once each night, Billy walked his rounds, covering four blocks of Main Street and the alleys on either side, to check the locks of the downtown businesses. Their front doors faced Main and their back doors faced the alley, where a simple thin knife blade would have opened most of them. The Pleasant Hour Lanes and Tables did plenty of late-hour business that left cash in the till; it had a twenty-five-dollar padlock on a hasp that a child could twist. A trained monkey with a tire iron could have broken in.

The bank would've been harder to break into. It needed a banker to do that. Matt Sorenstam had done it and flown himself away. No consequences.

THE MUSIC TEACHER and her lover drove into town on a Tuesday. It got out that they were married, a violation of Nebraska law. The ceremony had been performed in Mexico. The outraged half of Turtle Lodge formed a committee-of-the-whole in a certain church's basement to debate what a respectable town should do. The Hudspeths came up with their own answer: a shivaree. They would run the couple out of town and have fun doing it.

Somebody brought up that this was not the first instance of such a marriage. There had once been a settlement of black homesteaders, miles deep in the hills. Their sandy farms had failed and they'd moved on, but some of their descendants had blended into the community. Albert Watson had unacknowledged relatives.

No matter, said the Hudspeths. That was back in time forgotten. We need to give them an old-fashioned welcoming party.

Billy did not want to confront the Hudspeths; he liked them well enough, but not as adversaries. He had not signed on to stand in front of a steam roller or put out prairie fires. On the other hand, he couldn't afford to be seen as a pushover. It was his duty to keep the peace in Turtle Lodge, which meant he had to make a show of protecting the couple. To do nothing would cost him his job at a time when he needed the cover of his uniform. Once he lost its borrowed color of authority, any boy who happened to find his bayonet could make a convict of him.

Before that happens, I will kill again. Or else be killed.

It was a pledge that chilled his blood. Of killing Billy had seen more than a bellyful. Months, then years after Korea, he couldn't attend a war movie without shuddering; in dreams, he saw men mowed to death in hundreds, wheat before the sickle. Then there was Bernadette, skinny slip of wildrose beauty, snuffed out in one inexplicable moment. He'd smacked Gerard across the temple with force enough to kill a weaker man, and there were times when he wished he had indeed killed him. Other times, he felt relieved that he hadn't.

He thought of a small brown cur he'd shot, a pup with a scar where a chain had chafed its neck. It had run away from cruelty, to be brought to his hand and betrayed by a piece of chicken. Starved to a skeleton, it had gazed up at him with disbelieving gratitude. He had thrown the scrawny body under a bulldozer's blade out at the dump.

Some kind person should do the same for me.

Precisely at four o'clock, Billy got into his patrol car and started the engine. Then he shut it off and removed the ash tray and carried it to the trash barrel behind City Hall, where he dumped out Jonesey's foil-wrapped pellets of Spearmint. A wave of hatred washed through him that left him shaken. *Speaking of killing. What a worthless, stupid-ass excuse for a law officer.*

With the summer near solstice, it would be hours until sunset, and the afterglow would inhabit the northern sky until midnight. When the stars grew bright, that's when the shivaree would begin. Billy's part in the coming drama was not assigned; he had no role, no lines. He would have to make it up, and he had never been good at improvising. He couldn't count on prompting from Bernadette because she wrote her own script.

BILLY STAKED OUT the home of the two people he hated most, the Smiths, trucker father and trickster son. Therefore it did not simply happen that he was parked just up the street when the in-town McDonoughs, Rudy and Ellen, arrived and began carrying in groceries. Soon the miscegenated newlyweds showed up, escorted by George Smith. Billy watched them shuffle cars in the driveway and transfer packages. They carried suitcases into the house. Somebody had tipped them off about the shivaree, and they were closing ranks to prevent it. It felt as if a fissure was opening right in front of his eyes.

An imagined sequence of entrained events began to weave itself into a tapestry. He would walk in and arrest Albert Watson on suspicion of Bernadette's murder. If the Hudspeths chanced to learn of it, they might come to take Watson out of the lockup, and an altercation might follow during which anything could happen, such as a prisoner getting shot while trying to escape. The Bernadette Horse Looking case would be closed permanently, and Billy could go farther up the road and practice law enforcement, leaving Turtle Lodge's unprepossessing butte in the rear-view mirror.

"Were we not recently having a conversation about justice?" Bernadette.

"Shut up, damn you. Let me be. I'm trying to think."

Even if he only managed the arrest and nothing further—say the Hudspeths failed to take the bait, say Judge Brown declared a mistrial once again—things still might work out in his favor. The odor of blame would cling to Albert Watson. George Smith might suspect him, Billy, but Smith had little standing in the community, his war heroism forgotten since he was known to have aided Gerard. Ruth's son might piece the facts together, but he was only a kid and a nuisance kid at that. If Billy could get hold of the bayonet once again, hacksaw it into pieces and scatter them in the dump, any future case against him would have to proceed without physical evidence. And, speaking of evidence, there was a desk in the dispatcher's office with half a drawerful of hunting knives and switchblades, confiscated from various punks and drunks. Probably the drawer had not been inventoried in twenty years. There was surely a knife that could have stabbed somebody, one that would be easy to plant in Watson's apartment.

What if Baldwin had told his brother about the bayonet? Billy tried to shine the flashlight of reason. Number one, he did not know for certain who now held the bayonet; it could be anybody or nobody. Number two, the only way to connect Bernadette with the bayonet was to dig her up and measure the wound. Unless she'd been embalmed, which would have cost the county money, her corpse by now would be too decomposed.

Number three, nobody but Gerard had cared about her when she was alive, never mind that half the town wept at her funeral.

"You cared about me. Didn't you?" Bernadette again.

"I didn't, and I do not."

"You're lying, as usual. To yourself and everybody else."

God damn it, Billy thought. *Why can't the girl just leave me alone? And why am I such a pussy bastard anyway?*

Now that he knew where all of them were, he would come back later. There were baseball games scheduled at East City Park; first the Legion team, then the town team would play. Once both games were over and the dusty players hit the bar, that's when the trouble would start.

Lately, he'd focused on learning to use his target rifle, so that he hadn't kept up the required short-arm practice; his flashlight was all he needed for enforcement. Even so, he always strapped on the revolver, just in case. Now the holster weighed warm on his hip, like an over-friendly hand.

THE AMERICAN LEGION team lost, three to two. The town team played much better, trouncing the team from nearby Kensington nine to nought. Those who'd watched the game from their cars tooted their horns to celebrate the victory. As they left East City Park, dust rose in their headlights.

The vehicles leaving the game split into two groups. The first group of sedans and station wagons dispersed to go dead in their driveways and garages. The second group, mostly pickup trucks, headed for the downtown bars, although some continued to follow the L-shaped loop up and down Main Street and the highway. Billy's black-and-white circulated among slick cars driven by boys of high-school age; echoes off the town's brick storefronts amplified the blattering from their tailpipes. After half an hour he had had enough teenage nonsense. Either he could stop and arrest somebody, or he could pull his car out of the loop and let them do as they pleased.

Billy parked the patrol car half a block from George Smith's house. Light streamed through the screen door at the front of the house and spilled out onto the sidewalk; a Pontiac with Minnesota plates had replaced

Rudy McDonough's Dodge at the foot of the drive. Billy recognized the Pontiac with the out-of-state license; it belonged to Jack Keogh, now Turtle Lodge's banker. Jack Keogh's kid and Ruth's kid had been the two boys on the trestle who'd seen the music teacher when she jumped. They'd been fishing for the bayonet together. That brought Jack Keogh into the mix, practically the town's leading citizen.

"Jesus H. fucking Christ." Billy felt his lips peel back. He bristled like a coyote smelling a trap.

Billy knew the layout of the Smith house. The narrow little one-story had seven rooms, four of them in a line: Ruth's sewing room at the front—they'd screwed a few times there—then the living room and dining room joined, then the kitchen. A narrow entry at the front of the house lined up with the kitchen doorway, so that, on hot summer nights when every door stood open, a person looking in the back kitchen window could see right out through the screen door, all the way to the street.

The bathroom and two bedrooms sat off to one side. If he walked in through the front and approached the kitchen, that would leave three closed doors behind him. If he entered the kitchen from the driveway at the side, he would lose control of the situation because he'd have to ask to be let in. The screen back there had a hook to keep it closed and keep the mosquitoes out. He decided he would slip through a neighboring yard and scout the Smith house from the alley

As Billy stepped out of the patrol car, he felt his upper lip tingle and his knees go rubbery. It was the same surge of panic he'd felt as a young adolescent when Ruth got that hooded look in her eye. She had seemed grown-up to him then, but he now understood she'd been not much older than Bernadette. The hair that protected her teenage cunt had not yet coarsened and curled. Her body was slim and agile, her breasts small, white, and hard. Her stiff little acorn nipples had scalded his tongue.

The windows of the nearest house were blank; old people lived there. He exposed his dick to the cool night air and squeezed his eyelids shut until the colors swam. The summer darkness was warm and sweet, with fireflies sparking in the streetlights' shadows. He breathed in the dusty scent of hollyhocks, and for half a minute he was thirteen, in despair, in flames.

THREE MEN PLAYED cards in the kitchen: George Smith, Rudy McDonough, and Jack Keogh. The game, most likely pitch, involved the taking of tricks. The two women were not visible, nor was the mechanic Watson, though Watson's brown and beat-up car remained in the driveway. Billy watched for a while and concluded that Ellen must have taken the music teacher to the McDonoughs', leaving Watson under the men's protection. Where in the house the Negro bridegroom might be he could not tell. George Smith lit cigarette after cigarette. Rudy McDonough smoked, but fewer cigarettes than Smith. Jack Keogh did not smoke. Billy slipped back along the alley and returned to the street, passing the house with darkened windows where he'd left his sperm on the grass. He pictured Ruth as a skinny teenager on hands and knees, panties down, pretty ass at his disposal. *Never again*, he told himself, and the hot tears sprang. *Oh, never again.* He found his way to the patrol car, reached in through the driver's-side window, got hold of a tissue, and blew his snotty nose.

Might as well go in now and try to arrest Watson. George Smith will resist. So? Kill or be killed.

He made sure the revolver was loose in its holster and there was a live round in every chamber. He took his flashlight as well, because it had been a faithful friend and because they would think it strange if they saw him coming without it. He stumbled as he approached the driveway. A spray of gravel littered the concrete, so that his steps crunched as he passed between the bumpers of Watson's car and Jack Keogh's.

The first time he had entered Ruth's house, there had been a screen porch where the sewing room now was; the former sidewalk and step were still there, under one of the windows. He had come up on the train with his mother, who knocked and entered first. Somewhere inside, a baby was screaming, and the smell of diaper ammonia had almost choked him. The front room and dining room were less connected then, set off from one another by built-in bookcases. A row of ancient cedars loomed above the house, blocking light from the windows. Ruth lay in the dark in one of the bedrooms, with the crib by her bed. The sight of her was shocking; she had gained 30 pounds and become a different person. Her face held a guarded expression; there was no dry gleam of mischief in her slate-green eyes.

"So you came," she'd said to Billy's mom, ignoring Billy. Billy's mother had gone to the baby, picked it up and put it down, and gone off to look for a diaper or a kitchen towel. That left Billy standing helpless by the bed, gawking down at Ruth.

"Say something," she said. "Don't stand there breathing. You remind me of my husband."

"I'm g-glad to see you," Billy stammered. It felt like a lie. Her hair was matted, her face was pasty, and she smelled as if she hadn't washed for days.

"I don't care," she said. "I'm tired. I want everybody to go away."

"I brought you a present," he said, offering her a little box of expensive chocolates. "Don't tell Mom. I stole them from Kresge's."

"Get me some coffee," she said. "Anything else makes me want to throw up."

They'd stayed two weeks, during which time Billy barely had a chance to see her. Instead, he'd gone off with George Smith, who was driving fourteen hours a day, hauling cattle to the sale barn, then hauling them to Iowa. His mother had cleaned Ruth's house, done away with the pail of diapers, got the baby's rash cleared up, and got Ruth eating again. By the time they'd left, Billy's cousin was sitting up and his mother had showed George Smith how to make a decent plate of eggs. The last thing she did was lead Smith out to the driveway and point. "You need to cut those cedars down."

"I like 'em," Smith had protested. "For shade."

"Your wife needs sunlight," Billy's mother said. "Cut them down. This place is like a cave."

BILLY'S EARS RANG with the clink of aluminum as he pulled open the screen. He felt dizzy and untrustworthy, and his missing toe throbbed. The inner door to the living room stood ajar, and though the men playing cards should have heard him, they did not glance up. He soft-stepped the length of the front room and dining room, taking advantage of the thick nylon carpet, until he stood in the kitchen doorway. Still they had not seen him.

"Hello, fellows," he said, too conscious that he sounded like a fool.

George Smith looked up. A Springfield bolt-action rifle leaned against the window frame. Smith laid his cards face down and spread his fingers on top of them.

"I just stopped by to make sure there's no money on the table," Billy said. He swallowed thick saliva and tried a smile. "Is Albert Watson present?"

A rattling snore came from one of the bedrooms. "He is," George Smith said. "I think you just heard from him." A calculating look came into his dark-brown eyes. "Now, tell us again. What brings you here?"

"The vehicle of a known petty gambler is sitting in your driveway."

Now the other two men looked up at him. Billy saw that Jack Keogh was wearing a shoulder holster with a .32 automatic. The sight of Keogh wearing a pistol pushed him toward the edge of despair. He could shoot Smith and claim self-defense, but he couldn't touch the banker.

"You're not scouting for the shivaree party, then?" George Smith said.

"No. I'm not involved with that."

"You're supposed to be involved. You represent the law in Turtle Lodge, such as it is."

"I don't care." Billy felt a decade's worth of anger rising in his gorge. "I grew up in Lincoln, where they have a university. People don't do that type of hillbilly shit in Lincoln."

They listened to the snores coming from the bedroom and the quiet munching of gears in the clock above the stove. Now Rudy McDonough spoke. "There's no money, Billy," he said, and paused to stub out his cigarette. "But since you're here, we happen to have some business with you."

George Smith pushed his chair back and stood up. "Show you something, Billy." *Here it comes.* Billy tightened his grip on the flashlight. Smith stepped to the counter and opened a top cabinet, reaching high to lift a bayonet down from the shelf. He turned back to face them all and set the bayonet on the table. It wobbled a little because the blade was bent. "My son found it in that old Diamond T cab out at the truck barn. Looks like part of somebody's military collection. Fits a Russian weapon, as near as Starchy can figure. Their latest type of fully automatic carbine."

Rust had been scrubbed from the blade and it had been sharpened on a grinder. It was the kind of work a boy would do. Billy looked from one man to the other. If the three of them knew that the bayonet was his, Starchy Sedgwick would be in on it, and they must have told their women. If the women knew, then it might as well be in the newspaper. Billy's plan to frame Albert Watson went flying out the window.

Gerard Horse Looking was still a candidate. He might have got the bayonet from Billy's house. How then would it have ended up in the truck cab? *Think, man. Think.*

"About the only way it could've got to Dunlap County is by somebody who was in the Korean War," George Smith went on. "It hasn't been tested for fingerprints, but I suppose it could be."

"Let me see that," Billy whispered. His mouth had gone dry.

"I think I'd rather turn it over to the county attorney."

"It's evidence," Billy said. "I'm an officer of the law. Let me see it."

"Evidence of what? There hasn't been any stabbings out at my truck barn."

Billy glanced at Jack Keogh, then back at George Smith, who had taken Ruth from him and who now might take his freedom. "Gerard Horse Looking stabbed his sister. You helped him get away."

"There's no case pending against Gerard," Smith said. His dark eyes shone with malice. "Somebody did kill Bernadette, that's a fact. It happens I don't believe it was him."

Shit. Billy moved away from the doorframe. He needed time to think, but they weren't giving him any. He heard a footstep behind him, and the trucker's gaze shifted. "Son, you hadn't ought to point that at Constable Dixon," he said. The other two men at the table scooted themselves back out of the way.

"What are you doing?" Billy didn't take his eyes off Smith the father. "I'm an officer of the law. Are you threatening me?"

"My boy had a talk with Gerard the other day. Son, tell the constable what Mr. Horse Looking wants to ask him."

Now Billy risked a glance behind him. The kid was there, all right. He held a double-barreled 28-gauge quail gun that had once belonged to Ruth. His hands were steady.

Ruth's boy looked puzzled. "He wants to ask you why you broke his nose," he said to Billy. "He said he thought you were family."

For the blood. I needed his blood to mask Bernadette's. If Gerard understood why his nose had been broken, then Billy would not be safe, not even if he pled guilty and got sent away to Lincoln. Gerard could easily get himself sent to prison. The Dixons already there would not guarantee protection unless Billy paid them money. They had no family feeling.

Billy turned to confront the boy and his shotgun. The little turd had been the cause of his misery, all the way back to the beginning. If Ruth had never gotten herself pregnant—Billy pictured his .38 slug's impact, the boy's thin body blasted back against the doorframe. When, stroke by stroke, he erased that bloody picture, the face that emerged was Bernadette's. Ruth's features did not appear.

Behind him, George Smith spoke. "Constable Dixon wants to leave now, son. You are going to clear a path for him. I want you to stand at least six feet out of his way." If George Smith ordered his son to step six feet to the side, that meant that he wanted to remove him from the line of fire. A 1903 Springfield rifle was now trained on Billy.

Drop the flashlight. Grab the pistol grip. Half a second to clear the holster. The Springfield's bullet would strike his spine by then, but his dead hand might still shoot straight. Reflex action had saved him in the hills above Chosin. This boy whom he loathed was just fifteen feet away.

Two things happened, almost at the same time. First, Bernadette materialized beside the boy and placed her right hand on his left shoulder. Second, the mechanic, Watson, emerged from the bedroom, holding up a pair of boxer underwear that didn't fit. Watson came and laid his hand on Billy's arm as if there had been brotherly love between them.

"Come along, Billy. Let me walk you out of here."

Billy looked straight at Bernadette. Confess and go to prison, or kill and die; now would be the time to decide. He could probably plead to manslaughter, six or seven years at most. Once he got out, he could get a job with the Burlington. They didn't care what kind of men they hired to work on their track gang.

Bernadette reached across in front of the boy and tilted the barrels of Ruth's shotgun toward the ceiling. With Watson behind him, Billy walked out into the night, a free man and alive, with nowhere in the round green world to go.

Above the Roofs, Above the Water Tower

BILLY DIXON UNBUCKLED his belt and removed his boots. He kept his underwear and socks, along with the boots, but everything else he left on the seat of the patrol car, including his revolver, which belonged to the city of Turtle Lodge, and his uniform and flashlight, which he'd paid for himself. He laid his badge on the dash and left the keys in the ignition and walked home to his shoebox house. Two or three cars passed by the time he reached the dark streets south of the tracks. Each driver stared for a second and then looked the other way. He wore jockeys and a white T-shirt, and his long bare striding legs were as pale as cotton. The midnight air stirred the hair on his limbs and tingled his skin. He went home to the memory of his cat and his ghost of a girl. No one dead or living greeted him. Gerard Horse Looking's trailer stood empty. Now Gerard could have it back.

Bernadette was nowhere or anywhere—wherever it was she went when she wasn't mocking him. Billy put on his Marine Corps uniform, which still fit, though the pants were tight. He fixed himself a cup of Sanka and a thick cheese sandwich, and put the rest of the cheese and the loaf in a canvas backpack. Then he set his alarm for five a.m. and lay down to get some rest. He slept the blank sleep of the exhausted and woke up like a man who hears a gunshot. He punched the button on his alarm and sat up in the bed, and wondered for a second why he had his boots on. Armed men had been playing cards in the night. They had kept his bayonet.

The boy. The boy had had it all along. Ruth's boy had pointed her shotgun at him. He remembered: *I could have been killed.*

He could still leave town. In what? In his '49 Chevy that the newer V-8s had rendered a joke? To steal a faster car would only make his situation crazier. Besides, where would he go? Two highways led out of town, and one was just state-maintained gravel. It led to South Dakota in one direction and to miles of empty sandhills in the other. The dispatcher could head him off just by picking up the phone.

He could run, he could fight, or he could stay and bite his nails until he got arrested. Number one, no good; number two, no good; number three, no God-damned good.

"You're in a bit of a sweat, there, bucko." Bernadette.

"If you were me and had prison waiting for you, you'd be in a sweat yourself," Billy said. "Where have you been?"

"I've been having your baby." She turned her back and showed him the sleeping infant she carried in a cradleboard. (She wore a plain buckskin dress. The red coat was gone.) The baby had a shock of black hair like the crest of a cockatoo. Its eyes were closed and it was noisily sucking its fist.

Of course she claimed it was his, but given her brief wild history, it could have been anybody's. "I give up," Billy said, and indeed he felt himself weakening. "Tell me exactly what it is that you think I should do."

"Come up on the butte with me," she said. "We can talk about it there."

"Are we walking or driving?"

"You can drive to the foot of the butte. We have to walk to the top."

It required thirty minutes to load a few things in the Chevy: a shirt, ammunition, the backpack, his target rifle. He filled a gallon root-beer jug with water. He put in his pup tent and a blanket, though he could not see himself camping up there with the rattlesnakes. At the last minute he threw in a novel he hadn't finished, *The Far Country* by Nevil Shute.

"I'm ready."

At Bernadette's request, he drove them past the Smith house. All was dark and the front door was closed. Jack Keogh's Pontiac was gone. Billy felt a tumult of memories, good and bad, but Bernadette merely looked. He could tell nothing from her face. Billy himself chose to drive past the music teacher's. Here the smashed door opened into a shadowy wrecked interior. Torn sheet music and furniture stuffing littered the trampled grass.

"White people are strange," Bernadette said. "They think they own their houses, but the houses trap them. They can't just go whenever they want because their houses don't move."

"Would you rather be the slave to a house, or a slave of the wind?"

"We embrace the wind. We're not slaves to it," Bernadette said. "My relatives are a free people. Always have been."

"You were never free of hunger."

"There are many kinds of hunger. No one living under the sky can be free of them all."

They drove to the foot of the butte and parked near a broken picnic table. A trash barrel overflowed with cans and ammo cartons. Billy got out his pack and his rifle and the jug of water. "Should I bring the tent for the baby?" he asked. "How long will we be up there?"

"Don't bring it for the baby," she said. "I have everything I need."

Billy started up the trail; Bernadette followed. He climbed easily up the steep clay slope, his steps sure and agile. He'd been given an excellent body, and he'd taken care of it. Many women had admired it and they'd said so. The water jug sloshed awkwardly, but he carried the rifle as if he'd been born to it. The rapid climb made his heart and lungs expand; the early morning air felt harsh but sweet. They came out onto a prairie no bigger than a baseball diamond. Tiny flowers grew that were unknown in the vacant lots below.

A few scarred cedars and bur oaks defied the thunder. The floor was thickly sodded with buffalo grass and grama, so the rank grasses and Russian thistles could not come in. It would have made a perfect picnic ground if not for snakes.

"All the land was this high once," Billy commented. "The country you see around us was at this level. It took thousands and thousands of years to build it up like that, and it's taken wind and rain tens of thousands to wash it all away. If you dug straight down below your feet, you'd find the bones of elephants."

"That makes a good story," Bernadette said. "We've got stories of our own."

"I'd like to hear some of your stories."

"There'll be time for that."

Because it was summer, the sun rose north of east; the shadow of the flat-topped butte lay toward the town. They watched the streetlights blink out and the cars begin to move. The parking lot of the Milestone filled with coffee drinkers, and Billy imagined he smelled bacon frying. A parade of cars drove past the music teacher's house. Each car slowed as it passed, then speeded up again. Some drove around the block for a second look.

Billy ate a bit of bread and cheese and drank some water. Bernadette declined. He inspected his target rifle and wiped the dust off the barrel. His ghost wife took her ghostly infant off a little way to nurse, and he felt relief. It embarrassed him to have her follow him, even if no one saw them.

He sighted through the rifle's scope at the Milestone. The sheriff's wagon and two Highway Patrol cars sat in the lot. He wondered if his name had come up in their conversation. He wondered if he could put a bullet through a windshield at that distance.

He propped the rifle on his backpack with the barrel out of the dirt and lay back and put his hands behind his head. The sky above him was a crisp glass-marble blue, and the early sun slanted warm on his head and shoulders. The best thing about his constable job was not having to work in the mornings. He closed his eyes to better listen to a bobwhite's call and fell asleep.

BILLY WOKE TO the bell-like sound of young boys' voices. The sun through bur oak leaves was in his face; he must have slept for hours. He sat up and looked all around the top of the butte. Bernadette was nowhere to be seen. Below him, half a mile away and across the highway, some kids were playing ball. The way sound traveled upward was remarkable. He could hear an oriole singing in the town, and a woodpecker drumming on a light pole. Althea Dodson was probably calling the dispatcher to send the daytime constable, Jonesey, to scare it away.

Not me, Billy thought. *I don't chase woodpeckers any more.* Althea Dodson was somebody else's part-time job.

He picked up his rifle and sighted down at the ball field. Some of the boys he recognized; some he didn't. The pitcher was Keogh the banker's kid. Rosie Sorenstam's boy was playing third, which was odd because she rarely let him out of the house. Ruth's hare-lipped brat, Billy's enemy, played first base. Billy estimated the distance at about a thousand yards and tried to recall what the drop on a .30-06 round would be. He decided to target the Keogh kid first, so that if his round fell short or long (likely at that distance) it would strike the bare dirt of the infield. The puff the bullet kicked up would allow him to correct his aim.

His eyes remained open until the recoil slapped his shoulder. The crosshairs had wavered to his left as the firing pin dropped, and the bullet hit not far from the catcher, near the first-base line. Too high for the Keogh boy, about right for Ruth's kid; he'd forgotten that you had to aim low when you were shooting down. The boys didn't react to the bullet at first, but they began to run once the sound of the shot arrived. Ruth's kid screamed for them to not pile up at the gate, which of course was exactly what they did. Billy could have fired into the group of them, now that he had their range, and easily gotten one or two. Instead, he followed the tall first baseman as he sprinted diagonally across to the third-base side.

Billy's second round had no effect, though it felt on target. He saw Ruth's kid glance at the third-base dugout. "Still too high." Billy lined up the vertical crosshair on the boy and placed the horizontal marker below his feet. This time as he drew the trigger, something or someone deflected the barrel. He took his eye from the scope and looked up to see Bernadette standing next to him. "Damn it," he said to her. "You made me miss."

"It's no honor to shoot a boy at such a distance," Bernadette said. "You don't really want to kill him."

"How do you know what I want? Woman, get away from me."

"Besides, you can't. It's too late." The boy ran like a rabbit toward the bleachers, crossing Billy's line of fire. Billy sent a bullet in his direction by way of greeting, and took four rounds from the box and refilled his magazine.

The players that had jammed the gate on the first-base side had gotten through. Some hid behind an empty hot-dog wagon, but most of them joined Ruth's boy behind the grandstand. They were looking in the butte's direction, so they knew where the shots had come from. Billy spent ten minutes using up his ammo. He fired at shadows moving under the grandstand, though by now he didn't care if he hit a child or not. If there'd been a better target elsewhere, he might have tried for it.

Bernadette laid a hand on his shoulder. He stopped shooting. "Have you had enough?"

"There's one round left."

"Stand up and look."

Above them, a red-tailed hawk cried out. Billy got to his feet and shaded his eyes. The water tower, the ball field, and the trees and buildings of Turtle Lodge seemed to waver like weeds below the surface of a creek. The solid brick Milestone flattened out like a watercolor, and the cars in the parking lot grew shaggy hair and horns. A herd of bison grazed below the butte.

Next the bison themselves transformed. It was as if Billy's vision cleared and he could see beyond the horizon. An endless plain appeared, dotted with elk and bear and antelope. Nearby, a vast camp of people was on the move, men and women going on foot, with their dogs and horses loaded with belongings. There were mountain men among them, trappers like himself with muzzle-loading rifles. He lifted his arm in greeting, holding his target rifle in the air, and one, a red-haired giant of a man, waved back.

"I have to go," Bernadette said. "You need to make a decision."

"But—Ruth—"

"Forget Ruth. She's not coming."

Billy took off his combat boots and put on moccasins. Through the buckskin, he pinched his right foot, where the middle toe was missing. "Will it hurt this time?"

"It might. You won't remember it." He reached with his thumb for the trigger guard. The round cold muzzle pushed up awkwardly beneath his chin. "Don't tilt your head so far back," Bernadette said.

"You be quiet, woman," Billy growled. "I know how to do this."

"Of course you do," Bernadette said with a grin. "You're right. I'll be as silent as the stars."

ABOUT THE AUTHOR

Ezra Axelrod

Bob Ross (Robert E. Ross, not the painter) taught college English in six different states, most recently for nearly twenty years in Texas. He maintains a home in north central Nebraska, where he returns with his family every summer to read, write, think, and make repairs. From the autumn of 1972 to the summer of 1980, he lived on a sandhills ranch south of Long Pine, Nebraska, and it is during that time that he absorbed the coffee-shop lore that informs Billy and much of his work. He is a lover of birdsong, dogs, and literature that is not too difficult, most particularly the short novels of Anton Chekhov.

Other books by Bob Ross: *In the Kingdom of Grass* (essays, with photographer Margaret MacKichan) and *Solitary Confinement* (poems).

CPSIA information can be obtained
at www.ICGtesting.com
Printed in the USA
JSHW040826250321
12885JS00006B/13